THE CROSSING AT SWEET MAGNOLIA BAY

FRANK & EVIE

BLESSINGS HARBOR
BOOK ONE

JOSIE COLLINS

FAITH & FERN
PRESS

The Crossing at Sweet Magnolia Bay
Frank & Evie
Blessings Harbor 1
By Josie Collins

Copyright © 2025
Faith & Fern Press

For Mr. Sanders,
Your devotion and words are a gift to all.
Thank you for never giving up, and for the mittens.

WELCOME TO BLESSINGS HARBOR

The Crossing at Sweet Magnolia Bay

By Josie Collins

www.JosieCollins.com

PROLOGUE

There are places on this earth that hold magic in their very soil, where the Lord's hand has touched the ground with such tenderness that love seems to bloom as naturally as the trees gracing the shoreline. Sweet Magnolia Bay is one such place, nestled in the heart of what we've always called Blessings Harbor—though I reckon that name chose itself, the way the most beautiful things in life tend to do.

My grandmother used to say that every family story worth telling begins with a crossing—two paths meeting, two hearts choosing each other, two dreams becoming one. She'd sit on that wide wraparound porch of hers, the one that faces east toward the bay where the morning light dances like scattered diamonds on the water, and she'd tell me about the day my grandfather first saw her. How he knew, she said, from that very first moment that she was his home, and he was hers.

"A house is just wood and nails, sugar," she'd tell me, her weathered hands busy with some needlework or another, always creating something beautiful. "But a home—well, that's what happens when love walks through the front door and decides to stay."

The house at The Crossing has been many things over the years—a refuge, a sanctuary, a place where broken hearts come to heal and where new love takes root like the sweet peas that climb the garden trellises each spring. It has witnessed births and deaths, celebrations and sorrows, first steps and last breaths. But through it all, through every season and every generation, it has remained what it was always meant to be, a home built on faith, sustained by love, and blessed by grace.

They say that some places hold the echoes of all the prayers ever spoken within their walls, and I believe that's true of our home. You can feel it the moment you set foot on that front porch —the peace that comes from knowing you're exactly where you belong, surrounded by the kind of love that endures all things, believes all things, hopes all things.

This is the story of how it all began, how two young hearts found each other in the midst of life's storms and chose to build something beautiful together. It's the story of my grandfather Franklin and my grandmother Evie, whose love became the foundation upon which our entire family was built. But more than that, it's a testament to the truth that the Lord works all things together for good, even when we can't see His plan through our tears.

Every family has its legends, its stories passed down from mother to daughter like precious heirlooms. This is ours—the beginning of something beautiful, something lasting, something worth remembering. Because in the end, that's what love does. It creates stories worth telling, legacies worth preserving, and homes worth coming back to, no matter how far we roam.

So settle in, pour yourself some sweet tea, and let me tell you about the place where love learned to bloom. A magical place where two became one, and one became many, and where every sunset reminds us more blessings are on their way.

Welcome to The Crossing at Sweet Magnolia Bay, where many stories begin with the sort of Southern love that never ends.

CHAPTER 1

Blessings Harbor, 1969

"MOVE IT, EVIE, OR WE'RE GONNA MISS IT!" CALLIE'S VOICE carried from the school parking lot, her hem balanced on the window ledge of their father's hand-me-down Ford Falcon as her skirts bunched over the mint green door. Her other sister, Glory, tapped the horn repetitively as she waited behind the wheel.

"Late for what?" Evie called, her books weighing down her right arm as she hurried to the car. The June heat was already making her cotton blouse stick to her back, and the scent of magnolia blossoms hung heavy in the humid Georgia air.

"They're taking Perks and Blessings Cafe!"

Evie's steps faltered at the fender of the old Ford. "What on earth are you talking about? Who's taking it? And where?"

Callie's slender body slithered through the window and the door popped open as she scooted to the other side of the white leather seat. "Rawlin Landry, that's who! Now get in!"

5

As soon as the door shut, Glory gunned the car into drive. Pedestrians on an unhurried journey scowled and dodged the rambling vehicle in favor of safety over speed.

"Move along, people!" Glory called from behind the wheel, her voice carrying more enthusiasm than irritation.

"I don't understand." Evie fanned herself with her hand as the warm breeze whipped through the open windows. "How does someone take a cafe? There isn't far you can take a place cemented to the earth."

"Don't be silly, Evie," Callie drawled, balancing her elbows on the back of the front seat so she could stare out the wide windshield as Glory drove. Whoever gave her sister a driver's license should have been reported to the authorities. Evie remained safely in the back, her white-knuckled grip glued to the handle on the door.

"They aren't taking it anywhere. They're claiming it. Rawlin won it fair and square in a game of cards, and it's too good an opportunity to let slip away."

"You think Joe Perkins is going to just hand him the keys?" They were out of their minds, and Evie wasn't much in the mood for a Southern showdown on such a sticky afternoon.

Callie's grin was pure mischief, her eyes bright with excitement. "That's why Boone's going."

Evie rolled her eyes until she saw stars. "You think every Southern gentleman has connections. The only thing Boone Whitmore's good at is pronouncing grits properly and doing whatever his sweet mama wants."

"His mama wants him makin' a living for himself," Callie argued defensively. Chances were she'd end up marrying the dear man. There wasn't much Callie wanted that she didn't eventually get.

"Working as what, a server for Rawlin?"

"They're going to be partners, isn't that right Glory?"

"I don't know why you're fussing, Evie. They get this cafe, you'll finally have somewhere decent to get sweet tea and peach cobbler."

That was true, but not something Evie found remarkably persuasive. While her sisters were adults, she was still a seventeen-year-old senior in high school, but there wasn't much they did apart. While some girls went off to finishing school, her father was old-fashioned and of the mindset that a woman didn't need much more knowledge than how to change a diaper and follow a recipe.

It wasn't always fair, but it was all she'd known, and after seventeen years, she'd grown accustomed to his traditional ways. Evie didn't think herself overly qualified for things outside of the home anyway. Nor was she overly motivated to seek higher education.

She wanted one thing, and it wasn't part of any curriculum. She wanted to fall in love.

The tires squealed as her sister took the bend and yanked the wheel. Hand over hand, she directed the Falcon into Perks and Blessings Cafe's parking lot, where Spanish moss draped from the ancient live oaks like nature's own lace curtains.

"There's Boone," Callie sighed and fluffed the curls of her golden hair.

Glory slid the car into a slot and quickly adjusted her blouse. They sure did get ridiculous around boys—well, men. Boone was close to twenty-five years old, which wasn't too much of a difference considering her sisters were both in their twenties now. As far as age differences went, Evie sometimes wondered if she were an afterthought or a surprise to her parents.

"Who's that tall fellow?" Evie asked as they climbed out of the car, the humid air immediately wrapping around them like a warm embrace.

Callie blew a large bubble, the gum sweetening the dry May air. "That's Franklin Prescott. He and Boone are old friends. Good thing he brought him. Frank's built like an oak tree. Works for his daddy up at the dairy farm. Quiet sort of fellow, but he'll definitely provide the backbone we need if Joe Perkins tries to pull any nonsense." She blew another bubble and proceeded to chew thoughtfully as they approached the trio of men.

Evie's voice caught somewhere between her heart and her throat as she stared at the dark-haired man. The dark denim of his work jeans nearly matched the pressed navy cotton of his shirt. The sleeves were rolled casually up his thick, muscled arms, already bronzed in a way that told Evie he spent considerable time outdoors under the Georgia sun.

His collar was open, and his neck showed a hint of late-day shadow, something undeniably rugged, but she found it appealing for reasons she didn't understand. Her classmates didn't have that kind of presence. This was a man.

His hair was tousled by the coastal breeze, a collection of dark strands that looked like they'd been touched by Georgia sunshine. It was perfectly imperfect, and she couldn't help but covertly admire it. Her head remained tilted down as she studied him from under her lashes, her body facing Boone so her attention wasn't too obvious.

He grinned at something Boone said, but made no comment. While the others discussed the events that brought them there, this man remained pleasantly silent, like the calm center of a storm.

She found herself waiting for the slightest show of emotion. When he finally laughed, her heart seemed to leap into her throat as her palms suddenly grew damp. His teeth were perfect, his lips curved in genuine amusement. She'd never seen such handsome features. He was like a force of nature, beautiful in his own right, but commanding and deserving of respect.

Slowly, he turned, and Evie froze as two of the bluest eyes she'd ever seen rested on her. Breath turned warm and heavy in her lungs. With each slow pull, she became aware of her heart racing beneath her simple cotton dress. His lips curved into a gentle smile as he studied her. Her mind demanded she look away, but her body seemed frozen, literally held in place by that intense gaze.

The others continued to discuss their plan of claiming the cafe, but this man simply watched her. His attention, so focused and kind, became overwhelming, and she snapped her stare away, severing the connection.

But she still sensed his eyes on her. Like the warmth of sunshine that lingered even after stepping into shade, she felt him watching her. Nothing ever felt so wonderful and so nerve-wracking at the same time.

"Let's move," Rawlin said, his words finally penetrating her bewildered mind.

She turned and frowned as her sisters fell into step after the men. Reaching out, she grabbed Glory's sleeve. "You can't go in there with them. What if there's trouble?"

"Exactly," her sister said, grinning. "I don't plan on missing it. Wait here by the car and holler if you see the sheriff coming." She turned and followed the others inside.

They disappeared behind a green door painted the color of Spanish moss, and the parking lot fell silent except for the distant call of seagulls and the gentle rustle of palm fronds.

Evie frowned. They were a bunch of foolish dreamers. People didn't win cafes in card games. This sort of nonsense was exactly why her father grumbled every time Glory mentioned going out with Rawlin Landry. The man was a charmer who somehow managed to avoid settling down while others his age were long since married. Yet Glory adored him.

She'd once told Evie, "When I'm good and ready, I'll decide it's time for Rawlin to step up and be a man, and when I do, you can bet your boots his wandering ways will be over. Two things you should understand about life, Evie. There's divine intervention, and then there's the influence of a good woman. I may not have the power of good old-fashioned prayer, but I'm certainly no slouch when it comes to inspiration. Rawlin will do just fine."

Apparently, love was what motivated men to marry, according to her sisters. Evie wasn't entirely sure. Her father always said a man was incomplete without a wife, but once married, he was done. Their mother was a gentle woman, nurturing and always busy with needlework and cooking. Deep down, Evie believed their father loved their mother very much, but they rarely showed affection openly.

Evie didn't want that sort of love. She craved a love that was passionate and far too wonderful to keep inside. She wanted a love that held fast with bonds too strong to weaken over time.

The doors of the cafe burst open, and she jumped back a step as two men stumbled out, one wearing a torn shirt, the other walking with a slight limp. A ruckus of clattering dishes and raised voices sounded before the doors swung closed again. Lord have mercy, they were truly having words in there.

Glancing at the two men making their way to their car, she debated. It was inappropriate for her to enter the cafe, but her sisters were in there. "For the love of all that's holy," she muttered, tossing the keys onto the front seat of the Falcon.

Evie pressed through the green door of the cafe, unsure what to expect, but certain this was not typical. As though everything moved in slow motion, peaceful gospel music played softly from a radio in the corner as bodies moved around tables, men gesturing emphatically, and glasses clinked together. The aroma of fresh coffee and sweet tea filled the air, mixed with the scent of cornbread and fried chicken that made her stomach rumble.

Something sailed through the air, and the sharp sound of her sister's gasp caught her attention. Whipping around just in time to duck a flying sugar dispenser, she gasped and crouched low behind a table.

Her sisters were perched safely near the counter, Glory cheering Rawlin on as he gestured animatedly with Joe Perkins. Callie was speaking firmly to some poor fellow who'd made a grab for her hand and got a taste of her disapproval—the heel of her shoe likely making contact with his shin.

"Sheriff's coming!" someone called, and the discussion got more animated as everyone shuffled toward the doors.

It was complete chaos. Evie couldn't do more than stare as grown men argued with one hand and shook hands as they shouted to settle matters. Perhaps it was the lingering effects of recent conflicts that left them with such energy for debate. Or maybe it was just men being boys.

Music continued to play as the cafe bore the markings of a genuine disagreement. Though everyone seemed frustrated, they were also smiling the way stubborn Southerners often did when they were displeased.

A firm hand closed over her arm and she gasped, prepared to defend herself, but unsure how.

Dark blue eyes held her as his grip remained gentle but secure. "Come along, darlin', you don't need to be involved in this mess."

Breathless, she whispered, "But my sisters—"

"They'll be fine. Rawlin and Boone will see to them."

She shouldn't have gone with him, but those eyes of his seemed to cast a spell on her. Over the sound of animated voices and scraping chairs, she somehow stood, moving through the crowd and out of Perks and Blessings Cafe—holding none other than Franklin Prescott's strong hand.

His fingers enveloped hers as he pulled her close. The warmth of his broad chest steadied her as he guided her toward the door. His large palm rested protectively on her lower back, and for those few seconds, she felt completely safe.

Engines rumbled in the distance as the ruckus inside seemed to pour like spilled tea into the parking lot. "My truck's this way," he called as he led her toward an old black Chevy, clean but well-used. He reached the passenger door before her and opened it with a small smile. Not giving her a chance to climb in, he gently lifted her to the seat, and her heart took flight. "We should probably head out."

The truck thundered to life and she breathed in the pleasant scent of his cologne, something woodsy and clean like pine and cedar, before the smell of diesel filled the air. There was no chance for conversation during the ride through town. She was too stunned to speak anyway. Soon he was driving her down an unpaved road she'd never traveled before, past fields dotted with grazing cattle and farmhouses with wide front porches.

Her mind returned to her sisters, assuming the sheriff was now at the scene, asking questions. "Do you think anyone will get arrested?"

"You needn't worry about Glory and Callie. The sheriff will assume they're innocent based on the fact that they're ladies."

She chuckled. "I don't know that anyone's ever called Callie innocent. She might be uninvolved in whatever dispute they're having at the café, but my sister's always up to something."

He grinned, and her heart skipped as those blue eyes sparkled with amusement. "I believe you're right, but the sheriff doesn't know her the way we do."

"You know my sister?" It struck her as odd that Callie would know this man and never mention him. He was far more handsome than Rawlin or Boone. Perhaps that was the issue—his attractiveness put him out of reach and therefore not worth mentioning.

"I'd be remiss not to know the young lady my best friend plans to marry."

"Boone's going to marry Callie?" she nearly exclaimed.

He chuckled, the sound deep and pleasant. "If she'll have his sorry hide."

Although her father would be concerned, there was no doubt in her mind that Callie would eagerly agree to be Boone's wife. "When?"

Frank made a thoughtful sound. "Now, what kind of friend would I be if I told you that? If you're anything like your sisters, I'm certain you can't keep a secret to save your life."

Her stomach fluttered as they took another road she didn't recognize, past Spanish moss-draped trees and glimpses of Sweet Magnolia Bay shimmering in the distance. Something about him was stirring all sorts of carefully contained feelings inside of her, making her feel light and giddy as though she were a dandelion seed floating on the coastal breeze.

The question in her mind became too significant to ignore. "Do you have a girl—a young lady?"

"No."

His simple answer suggested it wasn't a subject he cared to explore, so she let it drop, though she couldn't help but hope that meant he was available. He was perhaps the most handsome man she'd set eyes on, not counting the fellows in magazines and such.

She rarely considered boys. They were childish and unappealing. However, she was only seventeen and far too young to set her sights on a man. Perhaps it was a result of having older sisters and spending time with their older friends that left her with a preference for maturity.

Either way, she'd figured, since Clark Gable was married now, she'd worry about meeting a husband once she came of age. Her eighteenth birthday was approaching, and now that she'd met Franklin Prescott, she was eager to reach adulthood faster, as if she could somehow catch up to him.

Straightening her shoulders, she drew in a breath and lifted her chin. Casually, she smoothed her skirt and waited for him to take notice.

He pulled into an empty, unpaved area marked only by a wooden fence. "We'll wait here for a while until things settle down. Then I'll take you back to your sisters."

She looked around, seeing nothing but trees and the fence line, catching the distant scent of honeysuckle and wild jasmine. "Is this private property?" No point in avoiding the sheriff only to be arrested for trespassing.

"Yes, but don't worry. It's Prescott property."

"You own this?"

He nodded.

"What is it?"

He studied her for a moment. "How old are you, Evie?"

It seemed important that she answer in a mature manner. No seventeen-and-eleven-months type response would do. "I'll be eighteen in July."

He made a thoughtful sound and nodded. "This is my family's dairy farm."

"You work here?" she asked, recalling what her sister mentioned.

"Been working here since I was a boy. Pop hasn't been well since the war. With so many men deployed, he's had a mess of issues and hardly anyone to help him run things." He glanced at her. "You probably don't want to hear about this."

On the contrary, she was fascinated that he was speaking to her at all. "No, please continue."

He shifted, draping his thick forearm over the wheel and facing her. It made her feel very important. "Pop never enlisted because he wasn't much one for combat. Said we saw enough war in the first half of the century that we didn't need any more. He was wrong, of course. I guess we all were, and when the world changed, he refused to change with it. I grew up on the farm, delivering water to my Pop and the workers and running their lunches out to them when my mama had them ready. Soon enough, they had me helping with the milking and marking pastures, because there was such a shortage of able men. When all the other men deployed, the work got more demanding."

"Do you like it?"

"Yes. I love being outdoors and enjoy doing things for my family. My mother looked to me as a man of the house. I liked the responsibility, too."

There was pride in his tone, something she respected and filed away as another appealing quality. If anything, Franklin Prescott was a capable fellow—no, man. He'd been a man far before the law would label him as such, and that was incredibly attractive.

"When my uncle died, Pop changed."

"Was he hurt in the war?" So many soldiers returned home missing limbs and bearing scars.

Frank touched his temple. "The war hurt his mind, even though he'd never once set foot on the front lines. Some bonds run so deep they might as well be wounds. My uncle and Pop had such a strong bond..." His head shook slowly. "He's never been quite the same since losing his brother. There's a pain inside of him too great to heal in this lifetime."

"I'm sorry." Once again, she felt her youth keenly. Her inability to offer comforting words left her feeling inadequate.

His head tilted, setting a dark strand of hair just beside his sharp eyebrow. His lashes were so thick she found herself wanting to reach out and touch them. "You don't have any brothers, do you?"

It was becoming difficult to concentrate on his words, but she desperately wanted to keep their conversation going. "No. Caldwells are mostly just blessed with girls." She laughed. "My poor father went gray before I was even born."

His smile was gentle, his eyes crinkling affectionately as if something she'd said pleased him. "You're a lovely girl, Evie Caldwell. I think I'm rather grateful your daddy was blessed with daughters."

Her breath caught as she stared at him, unsure if she'd imagined his words or if he'd actually said them. "How old are you, Franklin?"

"Twenty-five."

And there it was. Lowering her gaze, she casually smoothed her skirt back over her knee and folded her hands in her lap.

Though his accent was clearly Southern, his way of speaking reminded her so much of her grandmother. Words like "darlin'" and phrases like "blessed" were familiar and comforting, having heard them since childhood in the gentle cadence of coastal Georgia.

"Things have probably settled by now," he said, turning to face the wheel again.

Disappointment settled heavy in her chest as the truck started and they drove back to town in comfortable silence. It was foolish to think a man like Franklin Prescott would take an interest in a young girl like her. She'd be wise not to think of him in terms of attraction anymore.

When they reached the cafe, Callie grinned and met them at the truck. "I was wondering where you two had gotten off to."

"I didn't want your little sister getting hassled by the sheriff."

Evie tried not to flinch at the use of the word "little." "Where's Glory?"

"Inside. Cleaning up."

"What in the world is she cleaning up for? Did the sheriff blame her for this mess?"

Callie grinned. "Now, what kind of woman would she be not to help Rawlin straighten up their new cafe?"

"What? Joe Perkins actually gave it to him?"

"What choice did he have? The man owed Rawlin nearly fifteen thousand dollars."

Evie's eyes bulged at such a number. "From playing cards?"

"That's why they call it a gamble, Evie. He wasn't ever going to be able to pay that money back.

"But the cafe has to be worth far more than that," Evie argued. It didn't seem right to take the man's livelihood. The Perkins had owned Perks and Blessings café since the first magnolia tree was planted by the harbor.

Callie shrugged, clearly having reached the limit of her knowledge on the subject. "It's closed now if you want to go in. I'm waiting on Boone. Tell him to hurry along, will you?"

She and Frank entered the cafe, but he no longer held her hand or pressed his palm to the small of her back. He held the door for her, which she now found polite but not particularly meaningful. Their shoes crunched over broken glass.

"Watch your step, darlin'." His words provoked a sigh, but she stifled any moon-eyed response. He was too charming for his own good.

The place was in disarray, with overturned chairs and scattered napkins covering the floor like confetti. "I'm not sure it's worth a cent now," she mumbled.

"They'll have it cleaned up in no time."

Boone stood in the center of the mess. "Did you see the way I handled that fellow with arms the size of tree trunks and the big barrel chest? He was no match for me—"

"Boone," Frank called. "Callie's waiting outside and growing impatient."

That quickly, Boone's boastful tales ceased, and he was out the door like a well-trained pup. Evie shook her head at the control Callie had over that poor man.

Glory called from the back. "We'll be replacing those tables too. And this counter will need a fresh coat of paint. Are you listening, Rawlin? I won't be settling in until this cafe is right and proper, you remember that. Oh, there you are, Evie." She smiled. "Grab a broom from the back and start sweeping. We've got lots to do, and the mortgage is due by the fifteenth. Every minute those doors are closed we're losing money."

Evie stared, amazed, as her sister yanked the sign off the wall that had hung long enough to leave a permanent shadow on the paint.

"I think we should rename it Glory Grounds. Has a nice ring to it, don't you think?" Glory smiled.

Frank returned with two brooms and handed Evie one. She swept, in awe of what they were accomplishing and what it meant. It was a lot to process.

"Are you really going to move in with Rawlin, Glory?" she asked quietly as she swept alongside her sister.

She grinned. "I'm ready. I want to have babies, Evie. Could you imagine, us having our own sweet babies someday?"

"But you're not married." Their father would never allow it.

Glory's smile was the sort that spoke of many secrets and

warm affections shared between her and the man who held her heart. "Rawlin asked Daddy for permission last month, and he said we'd have his blessing if Rawlin could provide a home for us and find a way to make a decent living."

She wasn't sure about the cafe being decent, as it was won in a card game, nor was she clear on how this amounted to a proper home. "Will you live with his family?"

"No, silly. We'll live here. There's an apartment upstairs. It's nothing special, but we can stay there and save for a house. Down the line, maybe you or Callie could live there if needed. Since we own the deed, there's no rent."

Part of her was envious and thrilled for the sudden turn her sister's life was taking, but a greater part felt left behind. It was only a matter of time before Callie moved out of the house as well. She wanted to be happy for her sisters, but it was difficult to fully embrace such emotions when she was preoccupied with her own concerns. Her parents weren't the greatest company for those who didn't get excited about the nightly news or Gunsmoke.

By the time the damage was cleaned up, it was dark. There was still much to be repaired, but for the most part, the cafe seemed considerably nicer than when they'd first arrived. Frank disappeared sometime while she was wiping down chairs, and it hurt that he hadn't said goodbye.

It was getting late, and Glory seemed reluctant to leave when Rawlin was so devotedly inspecting his new enterprise. Begging for the keys, Evie took the Falcon home alone, something she imagined doing frequently in the future.

When she got home, the house was quiet, her parents each resting in their chairs in the den, the sound of crickets and night birds floating through the open windows. She quietly locked the door and went to her room at the corner of the first floor. Three twin beds. What would she do with all that empty space when the time came? She didn't want to think about it, but her mind wouldn't focus on much else.

She considered the friends she'd graduate with in two weeks and measured their appeal in matters of friendship, suitability as companions, and even potential company for summer activities. Did teenagers continue their friendships after graduation, or did summer become just another season?

Several of her classmates were scheduled for June weddings. While they'd been planning prom, others were choosing brides-maids and bouquets. The future was indeed daunting. The only skill beyond homemaking that Evie possessed was an ability to type forty words per minute. She'd likely spend the next year wasting away in some dreary office with a pathetic excuse for a window.

Before she fell asleep, she thought about the bluest sky her memory could conjure, comparing it in all its many shades and tones to the depths of Franklin Prescott's eyes. Though the sky could blush vibrant hues of pink and darken deeper than sapphires, she decided his eyes were victorious when it came to beauty, and she wondered when she'd be able to see them again.

CHAPTER 2

"It seems I'm always rescuing you, Evie Caldwell."

Evie blinked as her cheeks heated under the June sun. She'd been perfectly fine in the heat until Franklin Prescott pulled his truck behind her broken-down Ford. Now, warmth spread through her that had nothing to do with the weather.

"I hit a pothole and the whole tire burst."

Frank approached the rim and examined the damage. "You got a spare?"

"Maybe in the trunk." She disliked driving, and before Glory moved out, this was her sister's car.

Frank opened the trunk. "Nope. You in a hurry?"

It had been so long since she'd seen him, yet not a day passed that he didn't cross her mind. Fascination was an understatement.

"I'm supposed to be at practice in five minutes."

"Practice?"

"For graduation. It's tomorrow."

"Congratulations." He grinned, but his eyes told a different story. "I can get you a spare and have it fixed quickly, but if you don't want to miss practice, you'd better let me take you."

For some reason, her mind automatically calculated how many days until she became a legal adult. Unfortunately, every time she was in his presence, her mind turned to cotton and simple addition became impossible.

"Yes."

"Yes?" he asked with amusement, as though he found her breathless answer endearing. "Get your purse." She never knew what to expect from him. Though he seemed a man of few words, she treasured every one and never grew disappointed in what he had to say.

Grabbing her purse, she rolled up the windows. He waited by the open passenger door, and a thrill raced up her spine at the anticipation of him again helping her into the cab of his truck. He didn't disappoint, and this time she was prepared enough to appreciate the gentle strength of his hands around her waist.

Though she hadn't exerted herself, when the door closed, she was breathless. He climbed in beside her, and she found his familiar scent pleasing in too many ways. Her chest lifted as she drew in a deep breath, attempting to commit the unique fragrance to memory. Slightly dizzy from his nearness, she closed her eyes and silently sighed as warmth danced through her stomach.

He drove toward the high school, past the town square where Confederate jasmine climbed the courthouse walls and elderly men sat playing checkers in the shade. "You shouldn't be driving without a spare."

"Blame Callie. For all I know, she made a tire swing out of it."

He chuckled. "Are you excited to graduate?"

She shrugged. "I suppose."

"What will you do?"

Good question. "I don't know. I suppose I should have an idea by now."

"Well, think of what you enjoy and pursue that."

Her lips pursed. "That's a little difficult." Regrettably, they were already nearing the school.

Once he parked at the field, he turned and faced her. She sensed his expectation for her to meet his stare, but didn't have the courage to look into those haunting blue eyes.

"What is it you want, Evie?" he asked gently, and suddenly she felt as if he were asking about more than her choice of career.

She shrugged, no longer caring about arriving at practice on time. "I want to be loved."

"I see."

Slowly, with trembling courage, she faced him, wondering if Frank could somehow understand loneliness as well as she did. "Have you ever loved a woman?"

He nodded. "I loved my mother, but that's not what you're asking, is it, darlin'?"

"No." Where was his mother? He only spoke of her in the past tense.

"I think, when she died, she took a piece of my heart."

Her lips parted. "I didn't know... I'm sorry..." Her words stumbled and failed her.

"It's all right. The funeral was a few months ago and I'm... adjusting. My father on the other hand..."

Her hand instinctively went to his arm, her nature demanding she offer comfort. "I'm so sorry for your loss, Frank."

He nodded and looked at her hand. "You have a soft touch."

Her heart fluttered, and something warm settled in her stomach. However, when she looked at her bitten-down fingernails, she self-consciously curled them into her palm. "I try to grow my nails, but I'm always breaking them."

He glanced out the windshield, where many students gathered on the field as the teachers tried to organize them. "Do you not have someone, Evie? Is there not a young man you've set your heart on?"

Her hand slid away. "No. They're all spoken for or too childish to court a girl seriously."

When he stayed quiet, she glanced at his face and found him studying her again, a slight smile curving his lips.

"What is it?"

"I'm wondering if you're more like Glory, determined and spirited, or more like Callie, fearless and bold."

"Perhaps I'm neither. Perhaps I'm just Evie."

"Perhaps you are."

She didn't want to be like either sister. Not to him. She wanted him to see her, the real her. But even she was still trying to figure herself out.

"You'd better go."

"My car—"

"I'll see if I can get my hands on a spare, maybe find a tire swing with the right measurements." He laughed. "Then I'll meet you back here."

"Okay." If he was late, she could always get a ride home with someone else, but she hoped Frank was a man of his word and would be the only person driving her today.

He came around the truck and opened her door. Though he didn't lift her down, he did offer her a hand. When she took it, warmth traveled up her arm, and her heart raced. Moistening her dry lips, she stared at the ground. He didn't wear dress shoes like most men his age. On the contrary, he wore sturdy work boots that showed honest labor.

"I'll be back within the hour, darlin'. Don't worry. We'll fix the car."

Darlin'...

As the endearment met her ears, longing took hold of her like nothing she'd ever experienced before. She wanted him to court her, to hold her hand, to think of her as special. She trembled with hope for this man and felt uncertain how her feelings grew so strong when she'd decided not to be attracted to him.

"Evie."

Breathless, she looked into his eyes, but could not manage a single word.

"Go to practice," he instructed gently, and she nodded.

The truck pulled away as she stepped onto the field. She'd been so distracted, she'd left her purse on the seat, which was fine. It ensured she'd have to see him again.

"Who was that?" Barbara Geiges asked, balancing on her toes as she peered over the fence and watched Frank's truck disappear in the distance.

Evie frowned. "Put your eyes back where they belong and mind your own business."

She wasn't sure who was more shocked, her or all the girls now staring at her. Good gracious, where did those words come from?

Frank wasn't hers. Barbara had as much right to look at him as anyone else, yet the thought made her see red. She protectively wanted him to herself, knowing she didn't hold a candle to the other girl's beauty.

Evie was blessed with copper curls and more freckles than any person could count in a lifetime. Though her hazel eyes were pretty, they were overshadowed by her fair peaches and cream skin, and therefore the last thing anyone noticed about her—like two pretty stars in a poorly painted sky.

Too many times she'd wished to be exotically brunette or fashionably blonde. There were the Hepburns and the Monroes, among the sort of women men fancied. She was still waiting for trend-setting redheads to shift the way of the world, but none appeared. Apparently, Lucille Ball gave her kind a comedic reputation, but Evie was usually too shy to come up with anything funny to say.

Like most girls uncomfortable in their own skin, she depended on a healthy dose of wit and a good sense of humor to get her through the day, but that only worked around her sisters. Other people filled her with doubt, and most people assumed she was the quiet Caldwell. She had plenty to say, but no one besides Callie and Glory to listen, and now, they were leaving her.

Practice was a necessary bore, instructing her classmates to stand and sit like well-trained puppies. By the time it was over, her anticipation of seeing Frank nearly overwhelmed her.

Several people left to attend a party. School was officially over, the classes and final exams now concluded. It seemed only one ceremony separated her from the rest of the world and that thought was terrifying.

As drivers left the field parking lot shouting and honking with long-awaited joy, Evie's heart sank. She didn't see Frank's black truck. Glancing back, she spotted Barbara and several of the girls strolling off the field.

Embarrassment had her stepping into the shadows.

"Hiding from someone?"

A shiver spiked through her. His voice was deep and unmistakable, sending her heart racing like thunder in her chest.

Her breath caught as a smile crept over her lips. He came back. "I didn't see your truck."

He touched his lower lip as if tasting something there, and her attention was drawn to his strong jaw. "That's because I drove your car here. Couldn't have you riding off on a new tire without testing it out first."

His thoughtfulness and masculine consideration enchanted

her. Most modern women didn't care for such attention, finding it patronizing and old-fashioned. But Evie found it irresistible.

"Thank you."

They slowly strolled toward the Ford. "Did you want to grab something to eat? I know a small diner outside of town we could visit."

Was he suggesting they leave town because of their age difference, or was she reading too much into things, and he simply enjoyed the food?

"Sure, but I'll pay, since you fixed my tire."

"Not a chance," he said, opening the passenger door.

It struck her as odd that he'd drive her car. She was prepared to object, but as Barbara spotted them and stared, Evie simply smiled and slid into the passenger seat.

"This is a nice car."

"Thanks. It was my daddy's, then Callie's, then Glory's."

"And now it's yours," he said, smiling softly at her.

She worried about what his intentions were. Perhaps he was just a kind person, and this was all part of who he was. She decided dinner would be the perfect time to get to know him better.

When they reached the diner, he again held the door, and she suspected he would have pulled out her chair if they hadn't sat on stools at the counter. The place smelled of fried catfish and hush puppies, with sweet tea glasses sweating in the humid air.

"Are you going to be Boone's best man?" she asked, suddenly curious.

He placed the menu on the counter and turned to her. "Yes. And you..."

"I'm Callie's maid of honor, though it should really be Glory. She's paying for everything."

"It works out well that your family has the cafe now, since you seem to be hosting weddings regularly."

Glory's wedding would be a small, intimate affair, with only family in attendance. Callie's, on the other hand, was going to be large. Of course, hers would be at the same church where her sister and parents got married, but this time the guests would fill every pew. Callie always wanted a big celebration, and now she was getting one.

"I don't know if the cafe can hold all of Callie and Boone's guests."

"There's always a way. Don't forget there's a large field in the back, big enough for tents and tables."

True.

The waitress took their order and Frank sipped his sweet tea. "So, apart from wanting love, what else is it you're after, Evie?"

Every time he spoke her name her thoughts scattered like dandelion seeds. "I want a home to take care of, a family to love."

"So you want children then?"

"I imagine having a family would be nice," she agreed, not wanting to sound too eager or mistakenly presumptuous.

"I think you'd make a wonderful mother, Evie Caldwell."

She laughed. "How is that when you hardly know me?"

He studied her for a long moment. "You're gentle. Kind. You have a spirit inside of you looking to get out, and that red hair of yours tells me it's burning bright. Your hazel eyes hint at an adventurous soul, but I also sense a temper no wise man would challenge. But you're loving. I see it in the way you always consider others before yourself, wondering if your sisters are okay and doing whatever you can to lend a hand. I think you help others so much, it's probably why your nails never grow."

She glanced at her unkempt fingers and curled her hands into fists, hiding the short nails. His words amazed her. He'd seen so much in such a short time, which told her she wasn't mistaken and he'd been watching her indeed. "That's a lot of assumptions, Franklin Prescott."

"Am I wrong? Tell me I've misread you and I'll gladly apologize, but I don't think I have, darlin'."

She swallowed, something heavy weighing on her shoulders, countering the abundant hope she was already carrying for this man. "No, you're quite accurate."

The waitress delivered their food, but he made no move to eat. She was hungry, and his steady, accurate appraisal was making her nervous.

She frowned at the plate before her, as his burning stare heated her skin. "Stop staring and start eating before your food goes cold."

He chuckled, seemingly pleased at her boldness, and turned to eat.

After finishing the first half of his dinner, he asked, "How many children do you want, darlin'?"

His words caught her off guard, as they'd settled into comfortable silence. She wiped her mouth and considered the question. It was hard to say, being that she didn't have a man willing to marry her. "I suppose as many as the Lord provides."

"So you've got a strong faith?"

"Oh, yes, born and raised a believer. I've never missed a Sunday service."

"Is it the big church on Main Street your family attends?"

"Yes. My father's very active there."

He nodded and continued eating.

The meal was nearly finished when she recalled she wanted to find out more about him. He was skillful at turning conversations toward her and away from himself.

"Why don't you have a girlfriend, Frank?"

He shrugged. "I'm busy with work. Boone's going to take on responsibilities at the farm, which will help considerably, but until then, I have no time to court anyone."

She frowned. "But Boone's splitting the mortgage on Glory Grounds with Glory and Rawlin." Not to mention, with all that responsibility, Boone still found time to court her sister.

"Yes, and he'll pay that mortgage with his earnings at the farm. Rawlin will tend the cafe while your sisters serve customers, and if ever Boone needs more, the opportunities are there."

Again, she felt forgotten. "I wonder where I fit in."

His head tilted to the left. "Do you want to work, Evie? I figured you were the kind of woman who would prefer to stay at home, keeping house and family."

He hadn't made the role sound demeaning. On the contrary, his tone held great respect for a traditional life. "Was your mother a homemaker?"

"For the majority of her life. When times were difficult, she'd do side work here and there, sometimes she filled in at the office if they were between secretaries at the dairy."

She decided on honesty. "I think it would be wonderful to be a wife and mother, devoting all my time to a family and taking care of a deserving husband."

"I suppose finding a man deserving enough is what's slowing you down."

It was finding a man at all, but she didn't possess the courage to admit that. "Yes, I suppose."

He smiled, when she mimicked his gentle Southern drawl. "Caldwell. That's a good southern name."

"My mama's from County Cork. Daddy's family always lived in Blessings Harbor. He doesn't have quite the accent my mama does, but he doesn't say much either. She does most of the talking."

"My grandparents are primarily from Georgia, but my grandfather on my mother's side was rumored to be a northerner. I never met him, so we aren't sure, but the Prescott blood might have a touch of Yankee in it. That must be where I get my stubbornness."

Her chest lifted as she glanced at the counter, her face heating as her mouth curved into a smile. "And your parents? Are they stubborn?"

"Mama was always calm-tempered, unless she was upset. My father..." He shook his head. "It's been a while since I've heard his voice without bitterness clouding it. It's hard to recall how he spoke before the war."

Imagining Frank so estranged from his father, yet living under the same roof, was heartbreaking. Though she was not overly close with her parents, they spoke to each other every day, her mother more than her father. The longer she thought about her parents, the more she realized how her mother had been approaching her more often lately.

Perhaps, now that Glory was gone and Callie was hardly ever home, the house seemed lonely to her, too. Or maybe it was more of an attempt to finally build a friendship with her youngest daughter.

"What has you thinking so deeply, darlin'?"

"My mama. I suppose we are friends."

He nodded. "I considered my mother one of my dearest friends in the end. It gets easier as we get older. Don't be afraid to let her in."

Perhaps he was right. "Do you want children, Frank?"

"Yes. A houseful of them."

She laughed. "Well, from my understanding, the man has quite a demanding role in making that happen," she joked.

"From your understanding? Are you not sure, sugar?"

Her cheeks warmed as her lips pursed. She glanced at her plate, her stomach now full. "I've never..."

"Ah," he answered quietly. "I forget you're still young."

"Young, but not naive."

He frowned, and his easy posture shifted. "Never said you were."

Flustered, she stood and looked for her purse the moment the waitress cleared their plates away. He stood as well, his height both intimidating and appealing. "Where in the world is my purse?"

He caught her arm and tossed a few dollars on the counter. "It's in the truck and I told you you're not paying for dinner. Now, tell me what's suddenly got you so nervous."

Breathing roughly, her face tense as she met his steady gaze. "I suppose it's the obvious."

"Not obvious to me."

"Frank, you're seven years older than me, and I'm still in high school. I've never seen two people more unsuited, so I don't see a point in discussing family and such. It's all wishful thinking, and I don't need you dangling carrots in front of my face so you can get me to moon over you like some silly teenager."

She'd lost track of her words and he stared at her, his expression unreadable. "I don't think there's anything silly about the way you look at me, Evie Caldwell."

Emotion built inside of her like a volcano, and she struggled to keep it all in. Rolling her eyes, she sighed and left.

"Evie, wait a minute," he called gently, telling the waitress to keep the change.

Every word made her sound more like a child and she wanted to stop talking.

"Darlin', wait," he called as he met her by the car.

She reached for the handle of the driver's side door, but it was locked. As it refused to budge she broke another nail and grimaced, letting out a frustrated sound. "Give me the keys."

He grasped her shoulders gently, and she drew in a sharp breath, trembling. No man had ever held her so close.

"You worry too much," he whispered, his hands following her arms down to her wrists. Lifting her hand, he examined her fingers. "I had high hopes for that nail."

She'd never met anyone like him, so able to see into her ordinary life and find something interesting. He continued to hold her fingers, his warm breath sending chills up her spine. Her heart thundered, and she wondered if he could feel her pulse through the steady beating in her fingertips.

"You don't have to be nervous around me, sugar."

Her chest rose. "I don't know what it is you want?" she whispered, owning her naivety.

A gentle laugh escaped his throat as his eyes held hers, the fading light turning the deep blue into silver. "I thought I'd made it clear. I want to know you, Evie Caldwell."

She stepped back, but made it only an inch as the car blocked her way. He released her fingers and the soft jangle of metal filled the air as he produced her keys. Moving her gently aside, he led her to the passenger door once more, and somehow, she allowed him to reclaim control.

He wanted to know her.

What did that mean? Her heart? He wanted to court her? Or was it more than that? They were little more than strangers connected only by family and friends. Could it be possible that the emotions he stirred in her she also awakened in him? Perhaps her feelings weren't one-sided at all. Maybe it was something special.

They drove from the diner to where he'd left his truck in complete silence. When he pulled to the shoulder of the road, there were no other cars and she wondered how late it was. He put the car in park and faced her. She stared out the windshield at the dark taillights below his tailgate.

"When's that birthday of yours, darlin'?"

She frowned. "July twenty-fifth. Why?" Was he planning on getting her a present?

He nodded, making a thoughtful sound. "I'd like to call on you properly before then, if your daddy will allow it."

Her face turned toward him and she studied his sincere expression. Was this how a man asked to court a girl? "And if he won't allow it?"

"Then I'll wait until July twenty-sixth."

Her mouth curved into a smile as her eyes softened. "I'd like that very much."

His arm slowly reached across the distance separating them, cupping her jaw as he brushed his thumb over her lower lip, those enchanting blue eyes watching the journey of his finger. Her breath trembled as she stared at him. The windows were beginning to fog in the humid evening air. "I want to kiss you, Evie. And it's taking everything inside of me to hold back."

Nothing could be better for her in that moment than feeling his lips on hers. She was sure of it.

"You're tremblin', darlin'." He drew her closer, gently brushing the hair over her shoulder.

Her spine straightened as his breath skated over her cheek, igniting warmth in her bones. "Frank," she whispered, certain she should ask him to take her home, but wanting something entirely different.

His arms were welcoming, his hold warm. Chills chased over her shoulders and under her clothes. Her lashes drifted closed as he held her hand. Her breath quickened. She hadn't prepared for a moment like this.

As she waited for his mouth to brush hers, a low sound of appreciation left his throat, and he pulled her closer, his body pressing warmly to hers in a gentle hug.

"I enjoyed tonight," he whispered, his lips against her temple.

Her skin seemed to come alive under his touch. She never wanted him to let her go.

The car became warm, and she self-consciously looked around. Young couples made out in cars all the time.

He chuckled. "No, darlin'," he said, as if reading her mind. "It'll keep. I promise."

"Oh." Self-conscious, she returned to her seat and smoothed her hands over her hair as she glanced at her lap. Her dress was wrinkled, and her hair was slightly mussed. She'd have to fix her appearance before returning home, in case her father was still awake. She glanced at the mirror, shocked by how pink her cheeks had become.

"You're a dangerous girl, Evie."

Startled, she looked up at him with worry. "Why?"

"Because you make me forget myself."

She quickly looked away, a smile tugging at her lips, feeling more powerful than she could ever recall feeling before.

Again, he chuckled. "You're rather pleased with yourself."

Glancing back at him, she grinned. "No one's ever talked to me the way you do."

"And I'd prefer if we kept it that way."

"Franklin Prescott, are you staking some sort of claim on me?"

He nodded. "Yes, ma'am. And I'll expect you to remember my promise. I'll talk to your daddy the first chance I get."

A sharp thrill raced up her spine as his gaze turned protective. She smiled. "I will, so long as you remember your second promise." If her daddy said no, they would wait until she turned eighteen. Then, they wouldn't need anyone's permission.

"I will." He glanced at his watch and frowned. "It's getting late. What time's your ceremony tomorrow?"

Did he mean her graduation ceremony? "It starts at four. Why?"

"I'll be waiting for you at the edge of the field where the big sycamore grows."

Stunned he intended to attend her graduation, she beamed. "Okay."

He leaned forward and brushed his lips lightly across her forehead. "Good night, darlin'. You get home safe and sleep tight."

"Good night...Frank." She wanted to call him something endearing like *darlin'* or *dear*, but lacked the courage or creativity to think of anything special enough for a man like Franklin Prescott.

She missed him the moment he walked away from her car. The tail lights of his truck lit, and she slid across the bench seat to sit behind the wheel. He returned to her door, holding her purse.

"You'll be needing this."

She took the bag, electricity racing up her arm as their fingers brushed. "Thanks. And thank you for fixing my tire."

"Any time. Drive safe, now."

He waited for her to pull onto the road first, following her until she turned at the light in town. She watched as his lights panned across the bay in the distance. She didn't know anyone lived up by The Crossing, but now she was curious, curious about all things Franklin Prescott.

CHAPTER 3

Frank waited for the crowd to break up as he leaned against the trunk of the sycamore tree. Years passed since he'd last stood on that field, but memories of his own graduation seemed like yesterday.

He endured close to a dozen speeches and nearly six hundred names just to watch her receive her diploma. Though all the women wore the same emerald gowns, Evie wore it best. Her copper curls created a striking contrast to the dark green, her eyes vibrant under the green brim of her cap.

He was completely smitten. Typically he'd be ashamed at having such a reaction to a woman, but no one seemed to notice. His best friends, who would normally tease him mercilessly for such nonsense, were dealing with the same situation—all three of them under the spell of a Caldwell woman.

Poor Rawlin was buried with the undertaking of Glory Grounds Cafe, but Franklin didn't have sympathy to spare for the man. No, all his concern went strictly to Boone who was facing a life of matrimony to Evie's sister Callie. He loved the girl, but wouldn't marry her for a million dollars.

Evie was different from her sisters—sweet yet spirited. She intrigued him with just a smile and a quick flash of those sharp, grey eyes. Yes, he definitely entertained his fair share of thoughts about her, but he needed to temper his desires, at least until she turned eighteen. A girl like Evie Caldwell would likely save her virtue for her husband, but that wasn't a deterrent. He respected her values and saw her faith as part of her charm.

It pleased him that she was the marrying type. They seemed to share a fondness for traditional values. And, she was stunningly beautiful to boot. When he looked at her he saw life—a life he definitely wanted to grab hold of with both hands, knowing she could handle whatever came their way.

Cap gone, the flash of copper hair was easy to spot. He grinned and fluffed the blooms in the bouquet that wilted in the heat. The closer she came, the faster his heart beat until finally her hazel eyes met his and she smiled.

Turning to the woman next to her, she excused herself and slowly walked to him, her gown flowing in the gentle coastal breeze. She took his breath away faster than he could get it back. He wondered if he'd ever breathe right in her presence. Wondered if a man could go on living a lifetime of only shallow breaths ever filling his lungs.

"You came!" Her face wore a touch of rose from the sun that day.

"I promised I would. Here, I brought these for you." He held out the flowers, and her eyes went wide.

Slowly, she took the blooms. Her golden lashes lowered as she breathed in the soft fragrance. Her gaze returned to his and she smiled gently. "You're a sweet man, Frank. Thank you."

"It's an important day for you."

"Evie." Her expression turned apprehensive as her father called from about twenty paces away.

"You should probably return to your family," he suggested.

She hesitated, glancing over her shoulder at her mother and father. "Wait here."

Skipping off, he watched as she gestured expressively, likely asking her parents' permission to leave with friends. He wondered if the bouquet was a mistake. He'd yet to speak to her father, and the man didn't look too pleased to see him giving his daughter flowers and compliments, but he planned to act honorably and be upfront with his intentions.

Clearing his throat, he strode to where she spoke to her parents. "Pardon me, Mr. and Mrs. Caldwell. I wanted to introduce myself. I'm Franklin Prescott."

"Oh, I know who you are, son," her father said, eyes narrowing with suspicion. "What I don't know is what you think you're doing with my youngest daughter."

"Waylon," her mother gently scolded. "He's Callie's friend. I'm sure his intentions are good." Her accent carried traces of Evie's voice, stretching melodically with sweet Southern softness.

Her father eyed him prudently. "How old are you, son?"

"I'm twenty-five—"

"And my daughter is seventeen. You keep away from her, understand?"

Stepping back, regretting he'd botched such an important introduction, he glanced apologetically at Evie. Her brow creased, and her face flushed. He expected to see a sheen of tears in her eyes, but only fierceness stared back as she turned and scowled furiously at her father. "Daddy—"

"Say your goodbyes, Evie." Her father left no space for discussion. "We'll see you at the car."

Mr. and Mrs. Caldwell walked off and Evie stared after them, her hands balling into fists around the bouquet.

"I'm sorry," Frank said. "I only meant to—"

She quickly turned. "I'll meet you here in two hours. By then everyone will be gone."

"But your father said—"

"Are you going to fight for me or not, Franklin Prescott?"

"I don't want to fight your father, Evie. There are ways around this. Perhaps if I speak to him again—"

She waved away his words. "The man's as stubborn as a mule. If he gave Glory his blessing, he owes me the same. You're far more decent than Rawlin—taking that café from Joe Perkins the way he did."

"Perkins gave the café to him, fair and square, Evie. Nothing was stolen." Yet her father's rejection made him want to steal her, so he wasn't sure he'd call himself decent. "Maybe your father's right—"

"He's not. All you're asking for is a chance to court me. He'll have to accept that. In a few days, he won't have a choice."

Because by then she'd be an adult. But he was asking for much more than courtship and her father likely knew that. Gently, he clasped her chin in his fingertips. "You're a force to be reckoned with, Evie."

"I've never been known for my patience. My mother says I'm difficult."

He chuckled, amused by her shameless self-awareness. "You're clear about your convictions, and that makes it hard to tell you no." She was a temptation unlike any other. "All right. I'll meet you here in two hours, darlin'. We can talk more then."

She nodded and bustled away, flowers clutched in her hand, gown flaring behind her like a queen.

Honor battled with selfish desire, and he forced himself to walk away. For now.

CHAPTER 4

*L*ord have mercy, she'd be the death of him. He'd planned to speak rationally to her about waiting until she was an adult, but the moment he got to the field, she ran to him, throwing her arms around him, and somehow his mouth found hers.

It took several minutes for him to find the restraint to pull away, and even then, he wasn't sure why he'd bothered. "You're not familiar with the term playing hard to get, are you, darlin'?"

"I'd rather get what I want."

He led her to the fence, so they had somewhere to lean. "Did your father have much to say when you got home?"

"Nothing I haven't heard before. It was nice that you tried to speak to him today, even if things didn't turn out the way you wanted. I think someday he'll appreciate your effort."

He could only hope. "You look like your mother."

"I do. But I get my freckles from my father."

"I wonder if your children will have your coloring."

"I fear they'll have my temper." She smiled softly. "I think I'd

41

like boys with blue eyes and black hair." Her smile turned shy. "Maybe like their father."

Warmth spread in his chest as he pictured similar sons, perhaps a few daughters as well. "I think you'd make a fine wife, Evie Caldwell."

"And you haven't even tasted my cooking yet."

"My gut tells me it'll all be to my liking."

As their eyes met a thousand wishful thoughts seemed to pass between them. What was it about her that was so unlike every other woman? He loved her spirited nature balanced by her nurturing heart. To him, she was a perfect mix of all things feminine.

He was already dreaming about the next time he might see her. "How about a picnic tomorrow?"

"Don't you have work?" she asked.

"After work. Do you think you could cook something for me, darlin'?"

"What do you like?"

It had been so long since he'd experienced a home cooked meal made with love. "You decide. I trust your judgment."

She laughed. "Not a very wise thing to do, but I'll bring you something good."

The following day, he drove her to a secluded section of the harbor overlooking the bay where they wouldn't be disturbed. It was possibly a foolish move on his part, but he did it anyway. She'd packed a wicker basket and carried a plaid blanket over her arm.

He spread the blanket so half was in the shade of a weeping willow and half was in the late sun. Evie was indeed a gifted chef. As she unloaded containers, steam rose from savory cuts of turkey, fluffy stuffing, and hand whipped mashed potatoes. Everything tasted even better than it smelled.

He ate until he was stuffed and she seemed to take great pleasure in every bite he savored. "You're an amazing cook, darlin'."

"I'm glad you enjoyed it."

"Every bite." Lying on his back, he reached for her hand, pulling her to lay beside him as they gazed at the clouds in the fading pink sky. His fingers gently toyed with hers, and her head tilted.

"Why is it, when you touch me, I can barely think?" she asked.

"I feel the same. I don't know."

"Is it... did you find it was that way with other girls?"

"No. No one's ever had this effect on me before. You're one of a kind, darlin'."

Her mouth curved sweetly as a blush stole over her freckled cheeks. "You just like home-cooked food. I think I've put you in some sort of turkey trance."

He laughed. "Your food, your smile, your smart mouth, your curvy figure—"

She playfully swatted his shoulder.

"You've got a good figure, sugar. You can't deny it."

She looked back at the sky and let out a little huff. "My thighs are thicker than tree trunks, and my hips are too wide."

He frowned. "Your thighs are womanly, and your hips will be a blessing if you ever get that big family you want. Don't put yourself down. Words like that can steal your beauty faster than any physical flaw ever could. You're perfect, just as you are."

"Even with this hair?"

"Especially with that hair." He watched her for a moment, suspecting she was still silently degrading every beautiful part of herself. Why did women pick themselves apart so often?

"That's enough," he said, rolling to his side and turning her face so she looked at him. "I'll not have you pouting on such a pretty day."

The scent of nearby magnolias wafted sweetly in the breeze coming off the bay. He couldn't wait any longer. He needed to kiss her, then and there, so he slowly bent his head and brushed his lips gently over hers.

"That's a sure way to chase away my thoughts," she whispered.

"Then every time I see you look a little sad, I'll have to kiss you until you smile."

"Promise?"

"Promise." He kissed her again, longer this time, but pulled back before either of them got carried away.

In a trance, his fingers slowly combed through her hair. "You're the prettiest woman I've ever set eyes on, Evie."

"I am?"

"Yes," he said hoarsely. "I'm content to just stare at you. I want to learn every part of you. Know every secret hidden behind those watchful eyes."

"You just have to ask, and I'll probably tell you everything I know. It's not like I can think around you, especially when you look at me like that." She smiled softly. "I think I'd give you anything you asked me for."

"Anything?" His hand found hers, their fingers entwining as he gently clasped the ring finger of her left hand.

"Try me."

The thread of reality spun into a fantasy of hope, separating them from the rest of the world. When he was with her, she became his entire world, and he cared about nothing else.

"Aren't you afraid to marry someone you hardly know?"

She shrugged. "I'd think marriage would make you get to know someone better than any else ever could."

"What if I turned out to be the sort of man you didn't like?"

"I think the odds are in my favor. I'm no peach, after all."

"Ah, but I bet you're as sweet as one."

"Every peach has its tart spots." She laughed.

Everything inside of him wanted to run off with her and never come back. He'd never suffered such longing, such desire to cherish another person. "Are you saying you'd consider me?"

Her head fell back, and her fingers delicately toyed with his. "I'll marry you, Franklin Prescott, if you ask me to, that is."

His heart thundered so hard behind his ribs, it nearly knocked him out. "I'd make you a Prescott tomorrow if I could, but your father would never have it."

"In a month, his opinion won't matter."

He shook his head. "You're a good girl. Your father's opinion of you will always matter."

"Yes, but it's my life and I'm the one who has to live it. I'm falling in love with you, Frank, and I don't know how to stop myself."

The world stilled as her words sank into his soul. That's what this was. *Love*. How had he not realized that? "I'm falling in love with you, too, darlin'." Perhaps too fast for either of them to think rationally.

She shifted, coming to sit on her knees, as she looked at him with that mischievous glint in her eyes. "Let's get married, Frank. I know it's soon, but who cares? Plenty of girls my age get married. What good would it do to wait?"

Things were moving way too fast. He couldn't breathe, and his fingers tingled as though he were about to pass out.

"Now, hold on." He stood, putting some space between them so he could think. But all he thought about was how incredible it would be to have Evie as his wife. Pacing, he said, "We have to slow down, Evie. We're rushing things. You only just met me."

He wouldn't be panicking if such a large part of him weren't so eager to agree with her. Marrying in a fit of lust wasn't the responsible thing to do, and he should know better. But what if this wasn't lust? What if they truly were in love, and she was always meant to be his?

Soulmates.

"Wait for what?" She swung out her arms in frustration. "All my life, people told me to prepare for what comes after high school." "Well, here I am! What good am I? Sure, I can type and answer a telephone, but I'd rather spend forty years in the desert than sign up for a life sentence of fetching coffee and having orders barked at me by someone I don't love."

"But you'd sign up to a lifetime of cooking and keeping house, changing diapers and mending clothes?"

"Yes, because those things would be mine. It would be a commitment of love and devotion. What do I own if I'm only doing menial tasks for someone out of obligation?"

"You don't know if you'll feel that way in ten years. Women are different now. They want to work."

"And what happens in five years when I still feel the same and I've wasted time waiting for an unwanted epiphany. I know what I'm good at, Frank. I don't have many skills, but I know how to love, and Mama taught me that's all you need to know to be a good wife and mother."

He stared at her, not entirely trusting her certainty. She was young, too young to decide her life it seemed, yet he hadn't changed much since graduating either. Maybe she was right. "Do you also know how to bake?"

She laughed. "I can bake a cake that will bring you to your knees."

He chuckled. "I bet you can."

She glanced down and sighed. Shaking her head, she stood. "I don't want to marry you anyway."

"What?" After all that, she changed her mind?

"What good is a man that can't make a commitment? I need another indecisive person in my life like I need a third arm."

"Well maybe you'll be needing an extra arm since you're in such a rush to run off and start having babies! For crying out loud, Evie! I said we needed to slow down. Is it always all or nothing with you?"

She paused as if to consider his question. "Yes."

He dragged his palm over his face and groaned. "I'll marry you!"

She waved away his words. "Oh, forget it now. I can't have a man hemming and hawing about, deciding I'm only worth his future when the weather's just right and my father's in an agreeable mood." She stacked the dishes back in the basket and shook the dried grass clippings off the blanket. "You can take the leftovers home, but I want my containers back."

He gaped at her as she stood like an admiral about to go to battle over some storage dishes, the blanket now folded like a shield over her arm. "You're crazy."

"It's top of the line Tupperware."

"I don't give a care about the containers! I think you're certifiably insane."

She shrugged. "Maybe." She flicked another blade of grass from the blanket. "This will need to be washed."

He wanted to shake sense into her. One moment she was an enchantress and the next she was the most infuriating woman he'd ever stumbled across. How could any woman be that stubborn and rigid, decidedly set on something, only to change positions in the next breath?

She shut the basket and shoved it into his arms. "Here." She sniffled, face averted.

He took the basket and frowned. "Look at me."

"I don't want to look at you right now."

Dropping the basket to the grass, he reached her in half a step and turned her face. There, trembling above her golden lashes, was a wall of unshed tears. "You're upset."

She shook him off. "Don't be ridiculous. Upset over what? You?" She laughed. "I don't think so."

He grabbed her arm and pulled her close, not letting her escape this time. "You have tears in your eyes. Why?"

"Pollen."

"Liar."

"It's true. The air here is terrible. I must be allergic to magnolia trees." Her voice cracked, and his heart pinched.

"I didn't mean to upset you."

"Just judge me, I suppose," she said, crossing her arms.

"You mistake respect for judgment." He clasped her shoulders, thinking about her innocence, and the harshness of his words. "I'm sorry. I didn't mean to make you feel foolish."

"It doesn't matter."

"It does to me, Evie. I want you to trust me."

"I do. But you also need to trust me. Just because I'm younger than you does not mean I'm foolish and crazy for wanting the same sort of happiness everyone else seems free to find." Her words pitched with emotion. "I've thought about this. I've thought about you! Far more than you've probably ever thought about me."

"Hush." He pulled her into a hug. "I never meant to upset you."

She leaned into him, and his world returned to its axis again. "I forgive you."

It seemed wrong to love anyone so quickly and intensely. He tried to be skeptical. They barely knew each other, yet... he wanted forever with her, and his mind seemed set on that. How was that possible when he'd always been a man to make decisions slowly?

"You frighten me, Evie. I don't think it's normal for two people to fall in love this fast."

"If it were up to me, we'd go even faster."

Shaking his head, he said, "Women don't typically voice their romantic appetites the way you do, Evie. I don't know what to say when you say things like that to me."

"Oh, but it's okay for you to be saying you want to put your lips all over me?"

"I'm a man. It's different."

"That's another thing, Franklin. I may be the sort of woman who wants to stay at home and raise a family, but I refuse to live by some double standard. If you want to look at me, you can bet your boots I'll be looking right back. Being a woman doesn't make me any less human."

"Where on earth did you come from?" He'd thought Callie was the spirited one. Clearly he was wrong.

"Same place as you, Blessings Harbor."

It was getting dark and he was on the verge of losing his patience. The sight of her tears made him want to give in to all her wishes. "We have to be patient, Evie. I need you to be in agreement with me on that. I'd never forgive myself if one of those tears fell, so you have to understand my temperance has nothing to do with not wanting the same things you do. I'm just trying to do what's right here."

"I told you, it's allergies."

"Just be straight with me, darlin'. Can you trust me to know what's right?"

She was silent for a long moment, but nodded. "I warned you that I wasn't patient."

"That you did." He kissed her hair. "I promise, when the time's right, I'll ask you to be my wife."

She looked up at him and grinned. "Will that time be soon?"

"Evie—"

"What? I could talk a preacher to death, but you're quieter than a church mouse sometimes. For all I know, I'll be waiting ten years for a proposal."

"Hush now. It won't be that long."

She twisted her lips, and he saw the effort it took for her to trust him. "I'm just afraid I'll wake up one morning and you'll be gone."

"Where would I go?"

She shrugged. "Everyone's leaving these days."

Tipping her chin up he met her stare. "I promise you, I'm not going anywhere. Tell me you believe that."

She studied him for a long moment. "Is it too much to ask that you put it in writing?"

He laughed. There would never be a dull moment with her. "Is that what you need?"

When she nodded, he led her to the trunk of the willow tree and pulled out his knife. Choosing an area where the bark was somewhat smooth, he chiseled out their initials.

E.C. + F.P.
Forever

"WILL THAT SUFFICE?"

She smiled. "It will. Thank you." She leaned up and pressed a chaste kiss on his cheek.

Lord help him if he ever broke his promise.

CHAPTER 5

One morning, mid-July, Evie awoke with a sick feeling in her stomach. Her breakfast didn't sit well, and she later turned down lunch. After helping her mother around the house, she waited for Franklin to finish at the dairy farm, but no matter what she did, her stomach remained in knots.

"Do you want some ginger tea, sweet pea?" her mother asked, her drawl soft with concern.

"No. I'm not nauseous. I don't know what it is. Tension, maybe, but Lord knows what I have to be tense about."

"He does know, and soon enough, He'll tell you."

Her mother always claimed to have a bit of intuition, believing that most women possessed some sort of instinct. Evie was more likely to believe she suffered from indigestion. But then she heard the sirens.

Blessings Harbor was spread over a significant bit of land, but its population was small. When sirens rang, chances were you knew the person or place where they were heading. She quickly called her sisters to make sure everything was fine and then decided to take a ride. It was only natural to be curious when something happened in such a small community.

The sirens, which she'd decided had more of an ambulance sound than that of a police car or fire truck, wailed for some time before silencing. They seemed to have stopped by the bay, echoing against the coves tucked within the harbor. Every street she drove down showed no signs of distress.

Normally, she wouldn't care so much, but something told her not to stop searching. After an hour of driving around, she pulled into the lot at Glory Grounds Cafe and found her sister inside, working behind the counter with flour dusting her apron and the scent of fresh cornbread filling the air.

"Hey, Evie. Any news on the sirens?" Glory took inventory behind the counter.

"No. I drove all over town, but couldn't find where they were coming from. I need one of those scanners."

"The last thing you need is a way to interfere with the police. I'm sure we'll hear about it sooner or later. I just hope no one was hurt. I thought I heard an ambulance."

"Me too."

Glory shrugged. "So, how are things?"

"Wonderful, I guess."

She laughed. "You guess things are wonderful? Shouldn't you be sure before you upgrade from a general 'things are good'?"

"Can I have a sweet tea?"

"Sure." She filled a glass from the pitcher. "Have you been spending much time with Franklin?"

"Some. He works a lot. I'm stuck home with Mama all day. Maybe I should try to find work, because who knows how long I'll be waiting to get married and take care of a house of my own."

"Please. I can't listen to any more complaining about mothers. You should hear what Callie's going through. Boone's mother is a critical nightmare. If that mouthy Southern belle keeps it up, Callie may call off the wedding."

"But they're getting married in a week."

Glory shrugged. "A mother-in-law can make a bride rethink a wedding."

Evie frowned. Callie would never leave Boone. "Where's Rawlin?"

"He's in the back going over some bills. Things will be a lot easier once Callie and Boone are married and on the mortgage with us. You know, you could be a partner too. Maybe Franklin would like that."

"What does Franklin have to do with it? He's not my husband."

Her sister shook her head. "You're so impatient. I'll tell you I've known Franklin Prescott all my life, and I've never seen him take an interest in a girl like he's taken to you. But I've also seen him struggle to keep up with you. You don't have a filter, Evie. Franklin's quiet. He hardly ever says more than two words. Getting him to say the right words is gonna take some time, and forcing him is only going to make him clam up more."

"I'm not forcing him to do anything. He's the one with it in his head that we have to be married to be... close."

"I think that's sweet."

"Says the woman who's married."

Glory arched a brow and pursed her lips. "You're not even eighteen yet. Calm your burning loins, woman. Gracious."

Evie grumbled, crossing her arms. That was probably why her stomach was in knots.

The door suddenly burst open, startling both of them as Boone rushed in. "Where's Rawlin?"

"In the back. What's wrong?" Glory immediately came out from behind the counter.

"It's Franklin." He rushed toward the back of the café where the office hid. "Rawlin!"

Evie rushed off her stool and followed Boone to the back. "What about Franklin? Was there an accident at the dairy farm?"

The sirens...

Her stomach tightened as blood rushed from her face.

Boone's face paled at whatever Rawlin had said to him.

Evie panicked. "Someone tell me what happened to Franklin!"

Rawlin turned to her and swallowed. "His father took his own life," he said hoarsely. "He's gone. Franklin found him this afternoon."

Glory gasped and whispered a prayer. Evie grabbed onto a chair as her knees threatened to give out. *Why? Why did this happen?* He'd only just lost his mother. Should she go to him? She didn't know what to do, didn't know her place.

What did someone say in a situation like this?

Oh, Lord...

Suddenly, a burst of courage stiffened her spine, and the sickness that had plagued her all day faded away in place of fierce determination. "We have to go, Rawlin. He's all by himself at that house. I need you to take me there."

She didn't even know where his house was, only that it was somewhere by The Crossing on the bay.

"I think it's best if you wait here, Evie," Boone said, already following Rawlin out the door.

"But... I'm his..." Her words fell away. A terrible lump formed in her throat. "He only just buried his mother."

"Oh, honey." Glory pulled her into her arms and held her tight. "He's a strong man. He'll get through this."

Restless, she shouldered her sister off. "I need to go to him."

"Boone said—"

"I don't care. I know Frank. I need to—" Her lips clamped

tight. "I don't even know where he lives!" she cried, losing control of her emotions.

"Shh... we'll figure it out." Her sister nudged her into a chair and poured her a cup of coffee. "Drink that."

"I don't want it."

"Trust me. You do. I have a feeling this is going to be a long night."

She tried to lift the mug, but her hand shook too much to hold it steady, and she feared she might spill it. "What should I do, Glory? Tell me what grown women do in situations like this."

"Well," her sister started, pouring a cup for herself. "I suppose we cook. He'll be hurting, that's for sure. Rawlin said he struggled terribly after his mother died. We might as well make some casseroles to help comfort him."

Mothers always got the most love. Maybe that was why she wanted to be one so badly.

She sat with Glory until late that night, making grocery lists and pulling out old recipes. Rawlin called the cafe around nine, but the only report they got was that Franklin was *not well.* When Glory asked if he thought it might help for Evie to go to him, he said no.

It hurt, more than Evie would ever let the others know.

She refused to make this tragedy about herself, yet knowing he wanted his friends and not her, broke a part of her heart.

Franklin didn't have any brothers or sisters. He only had his friends. Evie couldn't imagine her life without Glory and Callie. Perhaps there would come a time when she'd want their company over Franklin's. She supposed confusing moments like this were all part of becoming an adult. Realizing not every aspect of adulthood would be free and fun gave her pause. She finally saw the value in a bit of patience.

If she didn't know how to handle moments like this, how

would she ever navigate marriage and parenthood? She'd likely mother the most headstrong girl Blessings Harbor ever knew, and shuddered at the thought. Maybe the Lord would let her practice on some easy children before giving her the difficult ones. Either way, she hoped Frank would be by her side so they could figure out the challenging parts of life together.

The following day, her mother helped her prepare one recipe after another. They worked in silence, Evie's worry taking her words away and hiding them far from her voice. Typically, she wasn't a quiet girl, but nothing seemed worth saying on a day like today.

As they wrapped up the dishes, her mother quietly asked, "Do you love this boy, Evie?"

She folded the foil over a dish of chicken casserole. "How do you know when it's love?"

"I suppose you just do. I think it's when you can't stomach the thought of a life without that person, but it might be different for everyone."

Evie used a marker to label the casserole. "Then yes. I love him very much."

"You know, your father will come around once you turn eighteen."

"I don't see what kind of difference six days will make."

Glory called that morning to say the funeral, a small, closed-casket affair, would be Friday morning. Callie and Boone's wedding was Saturday. And Sunday was her eighteenth birthday. She doubted anyone would be in the mood to celebrate, especially Franklin.

"That should do it," her mother announced, jarring up the last of the gravy. "You'll need a truck to deliver so much food."

"Thank you for helping me prepare all this, Mama."

Her mother smiled. "Of course, sweet pea. That's what family does. Do you want me to help you load it into the Ford?"

"No. I'm going to call Boone first to see if he thinks it's a good idea for me to drop it off."

"Why wouldn't it be? You're his friend. I'm sure he'd be relieved to see you, especially bearing supper."

She swallowed. "I guess you're right."

She didn't have the nerve to ask for directions, afraid Boone or Rawlin might talk her out of visiting. Rather, she drove to where Franklin carved their initials in the willow tree, and then let herself get lost from there. Several times she thought to give up, but she was too confused to find her way home. She couldn't quit if she wanted to.

Just as it was getting dark, she spotted a one-story house in the distance, small and in need of new siding. As she drove closer, she spotted Franklin's truck, and relief washed over her.

She parked beside his truck and used a handkerchief to blot some of the sweat off her nose. Though the sun was setting, it was still humid.

Deciding to leave the food in the car until she was sure he was home, she took the steps. The porch railing was rickety. The doorbell didn't seem to be working so she knocked.

Lace curtains blew in the windows, likely chosen by his mother. But no one peeked out. She knocked again. When he didn't answer, she called through the open window overlooking the porch. "Franklin?"

"What are you doing here?"

Startled, she gasped and turned to find him standing by her car. "I... wanted to see how you were doing."

"How do you think I'm doing?"

Her stomach shifted, and her head pinched with tension. Suddenly queasy, she reached for the railing and it shifted under her weight. Trembling, she folded her arms over her stomach. "I just thought…"

"You should go, Evie."

Tears stung her eyes. He was being so short with her. "I brought you some food."

"I'm not hungry."

"It's casseroles. You can freeze them for later. Mama and I spent all day making them. They're going to spoil if we don't move them to the icebox."

"Why are you doing this?"

She frowned. "Doing what?" It hurt that he could think she had some motive other than checking on him. "You need to eat, Franklin."

He shook his head, a cold laugh unlike anything she'd ever heard from him slipping past his lips. "Don't you see, Evie? The men in my family aren't well. My mother, I swear, she died of a broken heart. It didn't matter how much I loved her, my father never did."

"Your dad wasn't well, Franklin. And I'm sorry for that, but you're not him."

"Time will tell. I can give you all the sons in the world, but they'll never make up for a husband that fails you."

He was hurt and lashing out. She didn't want to drop to his level, but at the same time, his words were cruel and spiked her temper. "You're angry."

"I have a right to be."

She pressed her lips tight, biting her tongue. She had no idea what he was feeling in that moment, no experience remotely close to the tragedy he suffered. "We could pray—"

"I don't want to pray right now."

"Then I'll pray for you."

He held her stare, and she dared him to tell her not to. Clearly frustrated by her persistent stubbornness, he turned away and faced the bay.

He didn't want her there. "If you help me unload the food, I'll leave. But I'm not going to let all that good cooking go to waste." She marched past him and unlocked the trunk. Three boxes of casseroles filled the space. She reached for the lightest one, holding mostly gravies and sides. "Will you grab the big one? I'll get the door."

The crease in his brow smoothed. "You made all this for me?"

It was silly, but all she could think to do. "A man's gotta eat."

He nodded and picked up the largest box. The second she opened the door, her nose twitched with the urge to sneeze. It seemed their house hadn't been dusted since his mother passed. She followed him to the kitchen.

The home was nice, but small. Actually, it wasn't nice at all. She didn't know how to label it, but it felt vacant, hollow, as if it were once a home but somehow lost its soul. The dining room table was covered with paperwork.

"Are you working on something?"

"This is all my dad's stuff. Turns out he had some gambling problems. I'm trying to straighten a few things out, locate a couple deeds and such."

She sensed his tension and wondered if his father's bad habits affected the dairy business. Strange that he'd choose today of all days to go through such paperwork, but maybe he was desperate for a distraction. "Can I help?"

"No."

Her shoulders drooped with his fast rejection. She'd honestly wanted to do whatever she could to make this easier on him, but he didn't seem to want her assistance at all. "I'm sorry about your dad, Franklin."

He nodded once and remained silent.

He couldn't make it any clearer that he didn't want her there. "I'll get the last box and then I'll go."

"It's heavy. I'll get it."

"You're sure?"

He shot her a look and left her alone in the dusty dining room. Maybe she could clean it up for him. She'd be lying if she claimed not to be a little unsettled by the dusty clutter.

Without invitation, she went to the kitchen and opened the refrigerator. An empty plate and some milk were all that filled the shelves. This would never do.

She removed the plate and froze at the sight of dirty dishes piled in the sink. Filling the basin with water and soap, she let the mess soak.

"Your dishes are growing fur," she called when she heard the front door creak.

He placed the last box on the counter as she wiped out the fridge. The icebox really should be thawed and cleaned properly, but they needed to get those casseroles into the chilled air.

Once she had the food put away, she used the boxes for trash and found a dishrag and soap and got to washing. She didn't stop at the dishes and went onto the counters, cupboards, and walls. There were some charming patterns hidden under the dust that made her miss a woman she'd never met. She bet Franklin's mother was a sweet lady, and they would have gotten along nicely.

He never stopped her, just watched from the corner of the room as he sipped his sweet tea. She didn't mind so long as he stayed out of her way. She preheated the oven and pulled out a dish of green beans and ham.

Scrubbing the windows, she struggled to get the jammed locks open to let some fresh air into the house.

"Let me," he said as she pounded the heel of her palm on the stubborn frame. He grunted, gave it a knock, and the glass lifted.

"My hero."

He watched her, his eyes no longer scowling, but dark with something else.

"Where's your sweeper?"

He disappeared and returned a moment later, vacuum in hand.

"I'll be needing some lemon polish, too, if you have it."

She got to vacuuming, spending a great deal of time on the furniture. In the hutch, she found placemats and dishes, so she set the table. When the food was warm, the house was much tidier than she'd found it.

"Wash up. Supper's ready."

He dutifully scrubbed his hands and sat at the kitchen table, his head bowed over his plate long after she muttered through an awkward bout of grace.

"Do you not like green beans?"

His finger traced the eyelet pattern of the yellow placemat. "These were my mother's. I haven't seen them in a while."

"I'm sorry. I saw them and figured..." She stood, ready to remove the placemats. "I wasn't thinking."

He caught her wrist before she could take them away. His face lifted, and she stilled, finally seeing the pain he'd been hiding. "Thank you."

A confused smile wobbled across her lips. "I'm happy to take care of you, Frank."

Sadness haunted his eyes. "You have no idea what it means to me."

His gratitude filled her heart with warmth. She was starting to understand. Swallowing tightly, she let out a slow breath. "Well... let's eat before it gets cold."

They ate in silence. Franklin had three helpings. She wasn't sure how long it had been since he'd had a decent meal, but she was glad to satisfy his hunger. It was the least she could do.

After supper, she washed the dishes and returned them to the hutch. She found Franklin standing in the dark front yard when she was finished.

"I should be going."

His stare seemed fixated on the highest point of the harbor, across the bay in the distance. Nothing but wide-open space. She wondered how much of the land actually belonged to his family and thought it would be lovely to see a house overlooking the harbor someday.

He turned but held the distance. "Thank you again for the food and for...everything. You didn't have to do so much."

"It was my pleasure. If there's anything else you need..." She decided in that moment that if he asked her to stay she would.

"You should go."

Again, her heart tightened, but she told herself he was only creating distance in order to act honorably. "If that's what you want."

"More than anything, Evie, I don't want you to see me this way. I'm not good for anyone right now."

"That's not true, Frank."

He closed the distance, and for the first time that day, he touched her. She pressed her cheek into his gentle caress and closed her eyes.

"Please don't make this harder than it already is," he whispered.

Her heart broke for the pain hiding in his voice. Nodding, she decided not to push any harder than she already had. "Goodnight, Frank."

"Goodnight, Evie."

Accepting he wouldn't change his mind, she walked to her car and stilled. "Gracious." She bit her lip and stared over the dark crossing. "Can you tell me how to get to town?"

"Turn left at The Crossing and take that road for two miles."

She hesitated. "Will you call if you need anything?"

He gave a brief nod, but made no real promise. She knew he wouldn't call, and the next time she would see him would be at his father's funeral. In that moment, she desperately wanted to tell him that she loved him, but she feared more than anything that he wouldn't say it back.

CHAPTER 6

Frank stood at the head of his father's casket, stone-faced, as Pastor Mark said a few final words. Birds flew overhead, cars drove in the distance, as life went on, and one laid to rest. They were given roses to place on the grave. Frank looked so lost in that moment, an orphan on his own, amongst people who loved him, yet he refused to let anyone in.

Evie's chest tightened as her vision blurred. She clutched the yellow rose tightly to her chest before placing it on the coffin. Franklin didn't move. He simply stared at the gathering flowers holding his father's flag, his expression vacant of any emotion.

"Is there anything afterwards?" her mother whispered. "Prescott is Southern. There should be a gathering, no?"

"I don't think so, Mama." It would be inconsiderate to tell her mother that the funeral likely cost Franklin more than he could afford.

"Do you want me to wait for you, sweet pea?"

"No, I'll find a way home."

Her mother nodded and patted her arm.

People whispered condolences and quietly returned to their

cars. She glanced at Callie and Glory. Rawlin came to her side and whispered, "I asked him to come back to Glory Grounds with us, but he won't. Maybe you could talk some sense into him, Evie."

"Thank you, Rawlin. I'll see what I can do. Maybe we'll meet you down there."

He nodded and kissed her cheek. "Good luck."

Her sisters gave sad smiles and turned with the men toward the cars. The preacher left with the funeral director, and in the distance, men waited to bury the casket. She slowly approached Frank.

"What the preacher said was nice."

He only nodded.

She glanced at the men by the backhoe. "Do you want to go somewhere? We can go to Glory Grounds, or to a diner, or to your house, wherever you want."

He looked up, as if only then realizing that everyone had left. "It's over." He frowned. "Seems…abrupt."

There was a word.

She wrapped her hand around his and squeezed. "They didn't want to bother you, but they're only a phone call away if you want them to come back."

"No." He glanced at her, his eyes pained with denied grief. "You stayed."

"Of course I stayed. I'm your…"

His eyes met hers and his brow creased, but she had no idea what he was thinking.

"You can talk to me, Frank."

"I was just thinking, neither of my parents got to meet you. How does that seem the saddest part of all this?"

Her vision blurred as a lump formed in her throat. "I'm sorry, Franklin. I'm so sorry you have to feel this grief and suffer such a loss. I wish there was a way I could take some of the pain from you, but I don't know how. I feel so unprepared for this."

"You stayed. That means something." He tightened his grip on her hand. "Will you come home with me?"

Relieved he was letting her in, she nodded. "Yes, of course."

They walked to the car and drove to his house in silence. He was likely hungry. She hoped he'd left a casserole out to thaw; otherwise, dinner would be tricky. When they reached his home, there were more papers on the dining room table and a sink full of dishes. He'd been eating her food, and that made her happy.

He took off his suit jacket and draped it over a kitchen chair. She checked the fridge, but it was empty. Removing a casserole from the freezer, she started on the sink full of dishes.

"Don't bother with that."

"You have to eat. Once the sink's empty I'll fill it with warm water to speed up the thawing process. I can probably have you fed in a few hours," she explained, busily scrubbing what was filling the basin.

He stood behind her, his hands resting on her busy arms. "Is this what being married to you would be like?"

She smiled, warmth comforting her heart at such a fantasy. "Perhaps."

His lips pressed to her cheek. "It's nice."

The resounding truth that no one was home and this was now Franklin's house, continued to play on her nerves. "Why don't you go relax while I get dinner started?"

He chuckled. "Already giving orders like a good wife."

Normally, she'd scold him for such a comment, but he was only teasing. He kissed her cheek again, and released her. A few seconds later, the sound of the television kicked on. Was this what it would be like? It seemed so natural.

Once the glass dish of the casserole was soaking in warm

water, she abandoned the kitchen to find Franklin. He was sleeping on a chair in the den. A family show echoed from the set. Evie lowered the volume so he could rest.

She wandered through the house and stopped at the wedding picture in the hall. Franklin's mother was tiny. How did she manage such an enormous son? Again, patience seemed wise when it came to children.

Standing at the threshold of a bedroom, she noted the large bed and dated furniture. Deciding this was his father's room, she carefully shut the door.

The next bedroom was definitely Franklin's. The walls were orange and the carpet a hideous blend of browns. The bed was large and unmade. The furniture was nothing fancy, the largest piece dominated by a record player and speakers that were ridiculously huge.

Seeing his personal space made him seem more attainable. It showed shades of boyhood. She couldn't help but fix his bed. As she adjusted his pillows, she smiled, thinking of the sweet future they might share together.

"Making yourself at home?"

She jumped and turned to find him watching her from the doorway. "You scared me. I thought you were sleeping."

"I was. Thank you for fixing my bed."

Her cheeks heated at being caught in his private space. "I wanted to help."

"How long until dinner?"

"We have at least an hour before I can put the casserole in the oven. Then it has to cook."

He stepped closer, and her heart began to race. "Evie, I need to talk to you."

His serious tone worried her. "What is it?"

He took her hands in his, his blue eyes serious and intent. "You know I love you, Evie."

She stepped back, pulling her hand out of his grip. "Don't do this, Frank."

He frowned. "Why not?"

"Because I love you too. And whatever you're worried about, we can get through it."

"Evie—"

"No." She said indignantly. "I'm not letting you push me away that easily."

"Push you away? I'm trying to propose here."

"What?" She blinked at him, confused. "You are?"

"I know this isn't the most romantic timing, but losing my parents has made me realize how precious life is. How precious you are to me." He reclaimed her hands and looked into her eyes. "I love you, Evie. More than I ever thought it was possible to love someone else."

Her breath caught. "I love you, too."

"Then will you marry me? Will you be my wife?"

Tears sprang to her eyes as joy flooded her heart. "Yes! Oh, yes, Frank, I'll marry you!"

He pulled her into his arms, holding her close as they both laughed. When he finally pulled back to look at her, his eyes were bright with happiness despite the sadness of the day.

"I want to do this right," he said softly. "We'll have a proper engagement and a church wedding with your family there."

She nodded, her heart so full she could barely speak. "I'd like that very much."

"I don't have a ring yet, but I promise you'll have one soon."

"I don't need a ring to know you love me," she whispered.

He cupped her face gently. "You're going to be my wife."

"And you're going to be my husband."

They held each other close, both understanding that this moment—born from tragedy but filled with hope—would be one they'd remember forever. Despite all the pain, love found a way to shine through the darkness, giving them hope for a brighter future.

"We should tell your father," Franklin said, giving voice to her greatest worry.

"We will. But not tonight. Tonight is just for us."

They stayed up all night, planning their future and dreaming of the life they'd build together. Evie knew, whatever challenges lay ahead, their love would see them through. They were meant to be together, and soon the whole world would know it.

CHAPTER 7

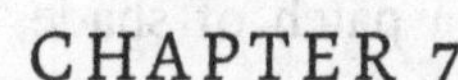

"You may kiss the bride."

As Callie and Boone sealed their nuptials, Evie watched Franklin, holding her breath for every subtle glance that ended with a flirtatious wink. At that moment, they seemed to have the biggest secret in Blessing Harbor, and it took all of her self-control not to shout it from the rooftops that she and Frank were going to marry.

The organ cried as the newlyweds led the way out of the church. Callie made a beautiful bride. Evie wasn't so sure about the yellow dresses she'd insisted the bridesmaids wear, but Franklin seemed to think she looked nice, so she supposed it wasn't too bad. Between the stiff lace collar, the puffy sleeves, and the frothy skirt dyed lemon yellow, Evie felt like a cupcake.

Outside of the church, the sun was beaming through the ancient oaks draped with Spanish moss. They'd sure earned a nice day.

"Evie, come take a picture with your sister," her mother called and she dutifully stood beside the bride.

Guests gathered on the church steps, tossing rice and congratulating the couple. Evie tried to imagine what such an event felt like as a bride, but she couldn't seem to summon the vision. She would be next, Franklin standing as her handsome husband, yet the image of them standing together on these steps eluded her.

Trying to escape to a patch of shade, she slipped out of the crowd. By Boone's car, decorated with ribbon and tin cans, she found Franklin and smiled. Though they'd been together all afternoon, she'd yet had a chance to speak to him alone.

He tipped his head toward a nook in the stone of the church where a basement door showed, and she followed him into the breezeway, her heart prancing at the chance to be alone with him. Stepping under the overhang, she grinned as he pressed a swift kiss to her cheek.

"You're a vision."

Forcing herself to pull back, she admired his tuxedo. "You're very handsome, yourself."

He pulled her closer, this time leaning in to kiss her lips.

"Evie!" She jumped at the hiss of her mother's voice. "Come out from there before Pastor Mark sees you, or worse, your father."

Elbowing Franklin in the ribs, she quickly went to her mother. "Sorry, Mama."

"What kind of woman kisses a man at church? It's a sacred place! Gracious, we'll be lucky if a bolt of lightning doesn't strike you down by day's end," she mumbled, bustling them back to the wedding party as they prepared for pictures.

The photographer was a snooty old man who acted as if he were being paid in pennies rather than dollars. Every shot seemed an inconvenience, and Evie wasn't sure why anyone would work as a wedding photographer if they disliked weddings so much.

"Just the men now," he called.

Thankfully, Callie decided to take pictures at the church, so they weren't in the heat. However, despite the fans and high windows, the air was still sweltering, especially with their fancy clothing.

"Now the parents of the bride and groom." Her mother and father walked to the front of the church, where Boone and his mother waited with his new bride.

Boone's mother was reed thin with the sharpest cheekbones Evie ever saw. Her shrewd eyes watched the photographer as her fingers, adorned with large ruby rings, smoothed her black hair.

The flash went off with a pop. "Now the groom and father of the bride."

"Oh no you don't," Boone's mother snapped, waving her bedazzled finger at the photographer. "I paid you good money to take good pictures, and I will not have one of me, my beautiful son, and his new family when I was not even looking." Her accent was a thick rolling rhythm of unbending insistence.

"The bride has a long list to get to—"

"And you'll get every single photograph, but you'll take them properly. Do it again, now."

Franklin chuckled and whispered in her ear. "That's why they call her Southern Belle. No one messes with Boone's mother."

Boone's mother was the sort of woman who dripped with saccharine sweetness, but phrases like *bless your heart* were never served in kindness. No matter how pretty her words, the woman spoke to everyone as if they were there to serve her. No wonder Callie was going crazy dealing with her new mother-in-law.

When the photographs were finally finished to Southern Belle's specifications, they traveled to Glory Grounds Cafe, where her family set up a feast out back. Much of the guests were already enjoying themselves by the time their father gave a Southern blessing.

There were far too many guests to sit comfortably anywhere,

but that made it a little easier to sneak away. Franklin caught her hand and pulled her behind a wide oak tree far enough away from the tents and guests that they could have a moment of peace.

Her breath hitched as he backed her against the wide trunk. "I keep wanting to kiss you, but we keep getting interrupted."

She hadn't been able to take her eyes off of him all day. He looked at her intensely and her stomach flipped. "Then kiss me now."

"Oh, I intend to, Evie Caldwell."

His lips brushed hers as she lifted to her toes, reaching for him. He kissed her sweetly, his hands gentle on her back in a way that made her feel safe and cherished.

Once he'd taken the edge off, he whispered, "I can't wait to make you my wife."

"Soon," she promised.

He chuckled and leaned close to kiss her again, except this time they were interrupted by Rawlin.

"You two better get back to the party. Evie's dad's looking for you."

"We'll be right there," Franklin grumbled, pressing his forehead to hers. "I need to speak to your dad. I don't like hiding our feelings like this."

She nodded. Everything would be a lot easier if they could be open about their relationship. "My mother doesn't seem to mind you."

"That helps."

When they returned to the party, everyone was dancing to the band Callie hired. "Perhaps now's a good time," Evie suggested as she spotted her father sitting alone, watching the others dance.

Franklin didn't look thrilled at the task. "Let's hope this goes better than last time." Giving her hand a squeeze, he let her go and walked to her father.

Evie watched as Franklin's posture took on a non-threatening presence, his hands hanging humbly at his side as he begged for her father's blessing. Her chest constricted as her father's brow creased. It was said she earned her stubbornness from her dad. There was no one more pigheaded than Waylon Caldwell.

When her father stood, nearly knocking his chair to the ground, she gasped. Stout and bow-legged, he still assumed a threatening presence. She knew Franklin failed when her father jabbed a thick finger at his chest and waved him away, ignoring his presence.

Franklin's head lowered as his shoulders drooped. Evie's teeth ground together as she scowled at her stubborn father and marched toward his table.

"Evie, don't," Franklin said, catching her arm, but she shook him off.

She stomped right to her father's side and demanded his attention. "Do I not deserve the same happiness you granted Callie and Glory?"

Her dad turned to her slowly, hardly investing an ounce of concern. "Your sister's wedding is not the time to discuss this, Evie."

She leaned close and hissed, "Is it too much to give me your blessing? Franklin is a good man. He's honorable and he loves me—"

"Honorable?" her father snapped. "Is he not the same man I forbade from seeing my underage daughter more than a month ago? What sort of honor is that, to go against my wishes? Now, you think you're in love with him when you're too young to know the meaning of the word."

His accusation infuriated her to the point of near tears. Tightening her lips, she stood up straight and whispered, "I do love him, Daddy. Tomorrow I'll be an adult, and we won't need your blessing." Her voice quavered. "I love you, but I love him too, and you can't get in the way of that."

"Evie, tomorrow may be your birthday, but you still live under my roof. Now that's enough of this nonsense. I'll have no more of this discussion. That man comes near you again, and I swear to Saint Peter, I'll aim my rifle at him. Now go see to your sister like you're supposed to be doing."

A sob worked its way up her throat, but she forced it back. She spun away and weaved through the cluster of finely dressed tables and abandoned chairs. Franklin called her name, but she ignored him.

Callie, dancing and laughing on the dance floor with her many guests, was in no need of her maid of honor. Her father just wanted to make her feel bad.

Choking back too many emotions, Evie kept her head down and lips tight until she found the exit. Pushing through the heavy doors with too much force, she placed her hands on her hips and let the door slam behind her.

Outside, the sky was dark and the air was muggy. The door opened and closed behind her as Franklin slowly approached.

"I'm sorry, darlin'. He's a stubborn man."

"He's unreasonable."

His hands rested on her shoulders as she stared into the night, fuming with impotent rage. "Give it time."

Her mind reeled with the need to escape. "Let's run away, Frank."

"What?"

"Take me somewhere, somewhere away from here."

"Evie, I can't—"

She grabbed his wrist and turned his watch into the moonlight. Eleven twenty-three. "I'll be an adult in less than an hour. It'll take them that long to even realize I'm gone. Take me away, Frank. I want to go somewhere I've never been, experience things I've never experienced. And I want to share those things with you."

His eyes creased with concern as he silently debated.

"Please, Franklin." Her vision blurred as she stared up at him. "I know what I want, and I'm tired of people assuming I'm too naive to choose what's right for me. You're right for me, more than anything else in this world. I love you. If you love me, take me away from here."

"All right, Evie. I'll take you away." He kissed her quickly and took her hand.

The thick evening air dampened her skin as they ran to his truck. He started the truck, and she grinned. She scooted close to him on the seat as he put the truck into drive.

"This dress is strangling me," she announced, snapping the pearl buttons at the back of her neck with a tug and tearing away the lace gauze choking her.

"You are a fearless woman, Evie."

She laughed and threw the lace collar out the window as they raced down Main Street. "Go faster, Franklin. Make it seem like we're flying."

He squeezed her hand as she rested her cheek on his shoulder. His foot pressed into the gas pedal as they sped away, flying off where no one could reach them.

CHAPTER 8

"Am I making a mistake, Glory?"

Her sister's sigh carried through the phone. "Do you love him, Evie? I mean *really* love him, so much so that when you're angry with him, that love will survive?"

She couldn't ever imagine being truly angry with Frank, but that was foolish. "When he drives me crazy, I still want him to hold me. Is that the same?"

"Not exactly, but maybe," her sister said.

Evie looked down at the dress she'd borrowed from the innkeeper of the boathouse. "I wish you could be here, you and Callie."

"See, honey, your mind's already made up."

She lightly ran her fingers over the fringe of a doily sitting under a message pad. "Do you think Daddy will ever forgive me?"

"You're his daughter. He'll have to." Her sister hesitated. "Evie, do you have any questions about being married?"

She bit her lip as her cheeks heated. "Will it be different? Living as husband and wife?"

"Everything will be different, but in the most wonderful way. You'll be building a life together, sharing everything. It's beautiful when it's with the right person."

She smiled. "I know in my heart Franklin's the right person for me."

"I think Franklin's a fine man and he'll make you a fine husband."

"Thank you, Glory. Truly." The innkeeper peeked her head into the office and nodded. "I have to go now. Tell Callie for me, when you see her."

"I will. Take care, dear. Call me tomorrow."

Setting the phone in the cradle, she looked at the innkeeper. "Is it time?"

The woman nodded. "Your groom is waiting for you."

Evie's legs trembled as she slowly stood. She was getting married, promising her life to another person until the day she died. She prayed the Lord would bless their union and help her be the wife Franklin deserved.

She paused to glance in the mirror. Her copper hair was braided around her head, baby's breath pinned in a crown. She hadn't thought to bring makeup, so her face was bare, wearing only her natural blush.

She'd cut a yellow strip of lace and used it to tie back some daisies she'd found growing on the edge of the property. They were in a small town about a hundred miles west of Blessings Harbor, surrounded by a large lake. Franklin discovered the town when purchasing a map from a gas station along the way. Apparently, the boathouse was a famous escape for lovers to visit and elope.

"I'm ready," she said, picking up her bouquet.

Following the innkeeper to the den, Evie steadied her breathing, but all bets were off the moment Franklin turned from the mantle and set eyes on her.

"My bride," he whispered, meeting her in the center of the room and gathering her hands. "You're as lovely as a summer rain."

She couldn't manage more than a smile, her nerves jangling like church bells. The officiant, a kindly minister, stepped forward. "Shall we begin?"

"Yes," Franklin said, holding her hand as they faced the mantle where wildflowers from the lake shore decorated the simple altar.

"Dearly beloved, we are gathered here today in the sight of God to join this man and this woman in holy matrimony. Marriage is a sacred covenant, blessed by our Lord, and not to be entered into lightly." The minister's voice was warm and reverent. "Franklin and Evie, as you stand before God today, remember that love is patient, love is kind. It bears all things, believes all things, hopes all things, endures all things."

Her fingers tightened around Franklin's as she felt the weight and beauty of the moment.

"Franklin Prescott, do you take Evie to be your wife, to love and to cherish, in sickness and in health, for richer or for poorer, for better or for worse, for as long as you both shall live, forsaking all others and keeping yourself only unto her, as God has ordained?"

His fingers squeezed hers as his voice rang strong and true. "I do."

"Evie Caldwell, do you take Franklin to be your husband, to love and to cherish, in sickness and in health, for richer or for poorer, for better or for worse, for as long as you both shall live, forsaking all others and keeping yourself only unto him, as God has ordained?"

Staring into his deep blue eyes, she whispered, "I do."

"The rings."

The innkeeper placed a box on the pedestal holding the two bands they'd selected from the display, Franklin's a simple gold band, hers with a small cross engraved on it.

"These rings are symbols of your unending love and commitment to one another and to God." He handed Franklin her ring. "Franklin, place this ring on Evie's finger and repeat after me."

The band slid over her knuckle, and Franklin repeated after the minister, his voice filled with emotion. "With this ring, I thee wed. As a symbol of my love and faithfulness, in the name of the Father, and of the Son, and of the Holy Spirit."

"Evie, place this ring on Franklin's finger and repeat after me."

Her fingers trembled as she slid the ring over Franklin's thick finger. She repeated, her voice barely above a whisper. "With this ring, I thee wed. As a symbol of my love and faithfulness, in the name of the Father, and of the Son, and of the Holy Spirit."

The minister smiled. "Let us pray. Heavenly Father, we ask Your blessing upon Franklin and Evie as they begin their journey as husband and wife. May their love be a reflection of Your love for us. Guide them, protect them, and help them to always seek You first in their marriage. Amen."

"Amen," they said together.

"By the power vested in me by God and the state of Georgia, I now pronounce you husband and wife. Franklin, you may kiss your bride."

Laughter nervously bubbled out of her as Franklin cupped her face gently. "My wife," he said softly, before placing the sweetest, most tender kiss on her lips.

Rising on her toes, she wrapped her arms around his neck and felt tears of joy slip down her cheeks. She belonged to him, and he belonged to her, and God had blessed their union.

"I love you, Evie Prescott," he whispered against her lips.

"I love you, too, my handsome husband. Forever and always."

The innkeeper poured two glasses of sparkling cider and congratulated them warmly. "To Mr. and Mrs. Prescott!"

They toasted their new marriage, and Evie couldn't stop smiling. She was eighteen now, married to the man of her dreams, and ready to start their life together.

"Would you like to take a walk?" Franklin asked. "There's a beautiful garden behind the inn."

"I'd love that."

They strolled through the gardens hand in hand, talking softly about their hopes and dreams for their future. The evening air was sweet with the scent of roses and jasmine, and the stars were beginning to twinkle overhead.

"I want to be a good husband to you, Evie," he said as they sat on a bench overlooking the lake. "I want to provide for you, protect you. Love you the way you deserve."

"And I want to be a good wife to you. I want to make our house a home, and give you everything you need."

He took her hands in his. "I know we rushed into this, but I don't have any doubts. Do you?"

She shook her head. "None at all. This feels right. Like it's exactly where we're supposed to be."

They talked until late into the night about everything and nothing—their childhoods, their faith, their hopes for the family they'd someday have. When they finally retired to their room, Franklin was the perfect gentleman, giving her privacy to change and settling on the small sofa by the window.

When she returned to the main room, he stood. "You're a vision."

Her blush seemed to rush to her toes. "I wasn't sure if this…"

"You're perfect." He closed the distance and gently kissed her.

Her nerves took longer than usual to settle, but in the end, Franklin was right. Everything was perfect.

The next morning, they had breakfast with the innkeeper and her husband, sharing stories and laughter. The older couple had been married for forty years and filled Franklin and Evie with wisdom about building a strong, God-centered marriage.

"The secret," the innkeeper's wife said with a twinkle in her eye, "is to remember that marriage isn't just about love, though that's important. It's about choosing each other every single day, putting God first, and never going to bed angry."

As they prepared to head back to Blessings Harbor, Evie felt ready to face whatever challenges awaited them. They had each other, they had their faith, and they had a love strong enough to weather any storm.

"Ready to go home, Mrs. Prescott?" Franklin asked, helping her into the truck.

She smiled at the sound of her new name. "Ready, Mr. Prescott." She couldn't wait to start a new life with him. Evie's heart was full of hope and joy. Whatever came next, they would face it together, as husband and wife, bound by a love that would last forever.

CHAPTER 9

On the journey back to Blessings Harbor, Franklin was quiet, and Evie sensed his worry about facing her father.

"He'll come around," she assured him. "Once he sees how happy we are, how much we love each other, he'll realize he was wrong."

"I hope you're right, darlin'. I don't want there to be a war between your family and us."

"There won't be. We'll make sure of it."

The closer they came to Blessings Harbor, the more Evie's elation turned to something unwelcome and frightening. Guilt, heavy and unpleasant, rested on her chest as she considered how her father might react. Chances were, he was already furious. She'd left her sister's wedding and not been home for two days, but little did he know that wasn't all she'd done.

"It'll be fine, Evie. Don't worry yourself sick. I'll talk to him."

She'd seen how her father reacted to Franklin's reasoning. "Maybe we should go to your house first."

"You'll be needing your things, darlin'."

When he wanted to be, her husband was quite unbending. It

frustrated her, but she knew he was right, and in a way, she respected him for it.

All she could imagine was packing her belongings in a suitcase that technically belonged to her parents. With every mile, it became more evident how unprepared she truly was for this moment. And though she'd done the most adult thing in her life, she never felt more like a child, her haste drastically discounting her maturity.

When they reached her street, she panicked. "I can't do this."

Franklin pulled over beside the large oak tree that shaded her bedroom. "Would you have us lie and say we're not married then?" He took her hands in his and kissed her knuckles. "The worst he can do is be cross with you, darlin'. I'm your husband now. I'll protect you and never leave your side. You won't bear the consequence alone, Evie—ever."

She swallowed and nodded. "You're right."

He walked to her door and helped her down from the truck. Back in her sister's bridesmaid gown, now wrinkled and in desperate need of laundering, she followed the path to the door. The screen door burst open, and her father stepped out, fire in his stormy eyes, pointing his rifle right at Franklin. "I'll thank you to take your hands off my daughter, boy."

Evie jumped, and Franklin blocked her with his body. "Sir—"

Her father cocked the gun and Evie yelled, "Lord have mercy, Daddy, put that gun away! Mama, Daddy's lost his mind!"

Her mother came rushing to the porch. "Gracious, Waylon!" She glanced apologetically at Evie and Franklin. "I thought I hid all his guns. Put that thing down before the police are called by the neighbors again!"

Her father, only a hop, a skip, and a jump away from being labeled certifiably unhinged, angled the rifle. "I warned you. For two days, you run off, and now look at you, coming home in shame."

"That's enough," Franklin said calmly, his fingers tight around hers.

"Evie, get in the house," her father snapped.

Breath sawed in and out of her lungs, and something inside of her snapped. "No, Daddy. I'm going with Franklin. I just came to get my things."

"If you choose to live a godless life——"

"Enough!" Franklin's eyes darkened as fury tightened his jaw. "You will not speak to my wife that way."

Her mother gasped, and her father paled, the rifle now aimed at the lawn. "What did you say?"

"You can criticize me all you like, but I'll not have you insult my wife. She's a good, God-fearing woman, and you have no right to speak to her in such terrible ways."

She was speechless.

The gun rose again. "Are you telling me you wed my daughter without my permission?"

"Daddy, we asked——"

"I'm not speaking to you!"

"With all due respect, sir, I asked for your permission."

"And I didn't provide it!"

"What's done is done," Franklin said, not a bit chastened.

"The union will be annulled——"

"No. She's my wife. We shared vows and we made our choice."

"Waylon," her mother whispered, but there was no getting through to him.

Evie glanced at her mother. "I'm sorry you couldn't be there."

Her mother carefully removed the gun from her father's grip

and his hands balled into fists. "Waylon, please. There are better ways."

Her father's jaw ticked as he eyed Franklin with icy fury. "One day, this will come back to you."

"Daddy, please."

His cold stare snapped to her. "If this is your choice, so be it. It's yours to live with." He turned and walked into the house, letting the screen door slam behind them.

Her vision blurred as her mother refused to leave the porch. "I'm sorry, Mama."

Her mother merely looked at her, a thousand words passing between them in silence. "You know where to find me, Evie." She turned and followed her father into the house, pulling the door closed quietly behind her.

Her spine seeped to collapse under the weight of their disappointment. Frank caught her in his arms, whispering promises that everything would be okay, promises even he couldn't guarantee.

He walked her back to the truck, pulled a kerchief out of his glove box, and blotted her eyes. "We just gotta give them time, darlin'. They'll come around."

She wasn't so sure.

The joy of matrimony was short-lived. She tried to recall her elation from that morning, but everything was different now. She knew it would be, but she'd never imagined anything quite so awful as seeing that look of disappointment in her father's eyes.

When they reached Franklin's house—without her belongings—she tried not to cringe. The place was not what anyone would call home. Misery tainted the doorway, and although the grass was brown, the sun never seemed to shine. It was impossible to imagine a life there, but this was where they were and all they had at the moment.

She held back as he helped her out of the truck. "You go on.

I'll catch up." She spent a solid minute convincing herself that any house could become a home. They just needed to pour love into it.

As he stepped onto the rickety porch, Franklin snatched a yellow piece of paper off the door. "What in the world?"

She looked up from where she stood on the scorched lawn. Plenty of small print filled the page, but even from where she stood she could make out the word printed boldly at the bottom of that yellow paper. *Foreclosure Notice. KEEP OUT.*

Her heart sank as Frank crumpled the paper and hissed out a prayer.

"I'm sure this is just some misunderstanding. If we go to the bank—"

"There's no misunderstanding. On top of skimming every profitable cent from the dairy business, my father was lousy at honoring his debts." He clenched the notice in his fist and laughed bitterly. "This should amuse your father."

There had to be someone they could talk to. Why should Franklin be responsible for his father's shortcomings?

"Let me talk to my mother. She'll talk some sense into my father, and we can stay there until things are figured out. I'm sure if you approach the bank and explain your father's passing, they'll give you a chance to square up his debt."

He looked at her then, not angry, but lost, much like he'd looked at her the day his father died. "Don't you see, Evie? They're foreclosing. That's months of debt. I was worried about making August's mortgage payment. I don't have the money to fix this amount of damage."

There had to be some way to make it right. "What about the dairy farm? Maybe you could use the property as collateral—"

"Only a portion belongs to me. The rest of The Crossing belongs to the family that owns the lake. I was hoping that Boone and I could buy more acres, but that was before I realized how messed up my father's finances were." He turned and paced away, coming to stand before the dilapidated siding as he fisted his hands on his hips and bowed his head in silence.

She jumped as he suddenly kicked the crooked railing. "Goodness!"

He kicked the broken post again, knocking it loose from the floorboards until the dry wood splintered. "No good, selfish, fool! You didn't take care of *her*! You didn't look after *me*! What good were you?"

Her heart broke as his anger unleashed on a deaf ghost. Helplessly, she watched as he raged, destroying the porch steps and expressing his frustration about his father. It wasn't right for him to face more hardships when he had been taking on responsibilities since he was a young boy. Where was the justice in that?

He drove himself into a sweat. Picking up a broken rail, he beat at the column barely supporting the awning. "You were never there for any of us! !And you're still making trouble from the grave!"

Evie's eyes glazed as tears blurred her vision. Her heart broke for him. How difficult it must be to be a man who wouldn't permit himself to cry. This rage was all his pride would allow. The wood snapped, and he threw it to the parched lawn, slamming his hand against the column and panting.

Once he seemed through, she slowly approached and rested a hand on his heaving shoulder. "We'll figure it out."

He shook his head. "I have nothing to offer you, Evie. I was a fool."

Her heart literally stuttered in her chest, his misguided sense of defeat terrified her. Didn't he understand her love came without condition? She didn't need fancy things or a house to be his wife. She only needed his love.

"You listen to me, Franklin Prescott. You have plenty to offer me. What use do I have for some rotted old floorboards and broken windows? This is just a shelter, and we can find that anywhere. It's love that makes a home, and so long as you love me, I have a place to live in your heart. I'll not sit here and listen to you put yourself down. Now, if you want my hand, I'm here, waiting to help you back on your feet. But beating the tar out of an already hurting house isn't going to do any good. I know you're angry with your father, and that's fine, but you don't need him and you don't need this house to have my love."

She was out of breath as she scowled at him. She didn't expect to snap at him, but it seemed the only way to get through his thick skull. She was sure the last thing he wanted was to be lectured, but he was acting hysterical and not thinking clearly.

He looked at her, his brow creased with confusion. "Where will we live?"

"You know how to work with your hands. Build us a house if that's what you need. Or," she emphasized. "You could focus on clearing up this debt and, once the bank's no longer threatening to take your land, we can rent a small apartment together like Glory and Rawlin."

"That'll take forever."

She nodded. It wasn't a quick solution, but what else could be done? She wasn't one to give up without a fight, not on something she wanted, and she'd never wanted anything as much as she desired a life with him.

"This is the perfect opportunity for me to learn some patience, since everyone's always telling me I need practice," she said, trying to get a smile out of him.

He took her hand, his fingers cut from his outburst. "I wanted our homecoming to be different."

"I know." She tsked and examined his fingers. "Look what you've done to yourself."

"I'm sorry I lost my temper," he whispered. "All I wanted was to be enough for you."

"You are enough, Franklin."

"We can't stay here, Evie."

"We'll go back to my parents."

He shook his head. "I can't face your father until I make this right. If he doesn't see me as a man, capable of providing for his daughter, he'll never approve of our marriage—and it is a marriage—a sacrament. I'll make this right for us, but I need some time."

"He'll see you trying."

"I'd rather show him me succeeding."

Her heart pinched as she understood they wouldn't be living together. "Where will you go?"

"I'll stay with Boone."

"But he's married now and they already live with his mother." It seemed horribly unfair that he'd be sleeping under the same roof as her sister, but not staying with her.

"Yes. Southern Belle will be a challenge, but at least she'll feed me well—"

"Don't you go lusting after some other woman's cooking. I don't care how old she is. You get excited about my food and that's it, you understand me?"

"Sorry, darlin'. It won't happen again," he quickly said. Then, in a more serious voice, he went on. "I can stay at Boone's tonight, and tomorrow I'll go to the bank to see how much my father owes. If I can prevent them from foreclosing and get them to agree to an extension, I think I can fix this in time."

"You'll come see me every day?"

"Yes. You can come see me too, at work."

She smiled, not having thought of that. Perhaps she could bring him lunch so he'd know her cooking was better than Southern Belle's. "I'll do that."

He nodded. "I best take you home now."

She didn't want to go, but he needed to make arrangements with Boone and Callie before it was too late, otherwise he'd be sleeping under the stars. "My sister will make sure you have a place to stay."

"Maybe your father was wise not to give us his blessing. He knew what kind of man Pop was, and he was only trying to protect you."

She gripped his shirt and tugged. "You are not your father, Franklin."

"I hope not."

"I know you're not." She pressed her lips to his. "Take me back to my parents and go see Boone."

He nodded. "I sorry about this, darlin'." There was a sadness to his eyes that scared her.

"None of this is your fault."

"Sure feels like it is."

"There's no point in placing blame. We need to focus on fixing things." Together, they could weather any storm, and any trials they faced would only make their love grow stronger. "You never know, Frank, this might just be a blessing in disguise."

CHAPTER 10

Franklin was, again, missing and Evie had enough. Getting in her car, she followed the dirt road up The Crossing to where she'd heard tractors running and men shouting. Boone and Franklin sat in the back of his truck with the flap down, eating something that looked like casserole. Scowling, she put the Falcon in park and grabbed his lunch.

When she slammed the car door, Boone looked up. "Uh... Franklin?"

Her husband turned and the smirk washed off his face. "Evie, what are you doing here?"

She threw the bagged lunch at him and he grunted as he caught it against his chest. "You invited me," she said firmly. "But I see you've already eaten."

"I'm gonna go check on that thing," Boone said, making his way over to the other workers.

"I've been busy—"

"You've been a coward!"

He drew back. "What?"

"I know what you're doing, trying to be the big man, bigger

than any pesky problem. Well, guess what, Franklin, hiding from your issues doesn't make them any less real. And how dare you lump me in with the problems you plan to ignore. I'm your wife, or have you forgotten?"

He came close to her face and said firmly, "I'm not hiding from anything."

"Liar."

They squared off for several solid seconds. "Go home, Evie," he finally said sternly.

"And where would that be, Franklin? My parents'? You do remember how to get there, don't you?"

"Last time I was there, your father aimed a rifle at me."

"That's no excuse! Where have you been? Five days, and I haven't seen hide nor hair of you!"

"I've been handling things."

She poked him in the chest. "You've been hiding."

"No. I've been thinking."

"About what?"

"Us!" he snapped. "A way to clean up this mess my father left. I spoke to the bank."

"And?"

His shoulders lifted and sagged. "I need to come up with ten thousand dollars to save the house."

Her hopes crashed as her anger deflated. "*Ten* thousand?"

"Yes," he said, with great futility. "I'm working late and doing everything I can, but I'll never make that. Not on their timeline." His pride was clearly hurt. "I don't expect you to understand."

His accusation stung, and she scowled at him. "Do not talk to me like I'm a child who doesn't understand, Franklin."

It seemed they were at an impasse, both hurting and too lost in the pain to appreciate the ways they might comfort each other through such challenges. He feared he was losing his identity, and she was trying to find hers. But the tighter he held onto the past the more he seemed to push her away.

"I'm losing him," she told her sisters later that night."

"He's been working his tail off trying to make that money, Evie. The man's tense, and he isn't living with his wife. The stress has to be getting to him. He needs an outlet," Callie explained, brimming with untested marital wisdom.

Evie grumbled into her sweet tea. "Married a day longer than me, and you think you've got the market cornered when it comes to matrimony."

"I have more experience," Callie argued.

Evie scowled. "You live at your mother-in-law's house in Boone's childhood bedroom. What do you know?"

"I know how to keep my husband's temper in hand." Her sister arched a brow, and she and Glory rolled their eyes.

"Listen to me," Glory whispered, leaning over the counter. " A Southern man's got more pride than common sense. Franklin loves you. He's trying to figure out a way to make a home for you so you can have a right and proper marriage. He hasn't said much to Rawlin, but I know he wants Daddy's approval. Like I said, it's a matter of pride."

"All that pride sounds like a hassle to me," Callie mumbled.

"Hush," Glory snapped "I wasn't talking to you," Softening her tone, she turned back to Evie. "Give him time."

Evie was terrified her marriage was over before it even began. Her face lowered and she shut her eyes. Quietly, she whispered, "He's breaking my heart."

He sisters met her confession with silence. There was nothing they could do or say to take away the fact that his distance was destroying her.

· · ·

WHAT WAS HE GOING TO DO?

"Lord help me," Franklin prayed, as he walked the property line under the setting sun.

He'd made a terrible mistake. Evie deserved a husband who could take care of her.

He frowned into the fading sky. No options left. No home to shelter his wife and no money to put food on the table when everything he made went toward his father's debts.

A night owl screeched from somewhere in The Crossing. He walked toward the weeping willow tree, trailing his hand along the bark until his fingers dragged over the rigid carving where their initials were inscribed above the word forever.

What a joke. He was losing her. Mostly, because he didn't deserve her. He should never have trapped her in this sham of a marriage. She was too good. Too beautiful. And he had absolutely nothing to offer her besides an endless debt and a bad name.

His chest tightened. He didn't want to let her go, but what choice did he have? He couldn't take care of her the way a husband should. He would not sentence her to a life of struggle and neglect like his father had done to his mother. She was still young. She could start over.

He stared over The Crossing at the distance at the inky sky. Her father was right. They should have listened to him.

By the time he'd walked back to his truck, he knew what he had to do. She'd likely put up a fight, probably slap him once or twice, too. He wouldn't hold it against her if she did. Maybe if she hated him, this would be easier and she'd move on faster. It would be for the best.

His gut swirled uncomfortably at the thought. He hated the idea of her with anyone but him, but he couldn't expect her to wait around forever for her life to start. She deserved a good life, one that was stable and secure. One where she could have the family she dreamed of.

When he reached her house, he decided to go right to her father. He'd apologize, hat in hand, and try to make this right.

Reluctantly, he climbed out of his truck. Bushes rustled, and there was a sharp yelp. "Gracious!"

He frowned at the rustling hedge. "Evie?"

The bushes shifted, and she emerged from the branches, a twig stuck in her hair and a smudge of dirt on her cheek. She smiled and whispered, "You came!"

She was in a nightgown. "Where are you coming from, woman?"

"What? Oh. I climbed out the window. My parents are sleeping. I didn't want you to wake them. Every night I wait by the window, hoping you'll visit."

Guilt knifed through him as she closed the distance and hugged him. Had she really been waiting for him night after night?

He couldn't let her devotion sway him from the task at hand. Setting her back a step, he said, "I need to speak to your father."

She frowned. "Why? Did something happen with the bank?"

This was harder than he expected.

She closed the distance again, her nearness a persistent distraction that muddled his purpose. "Evie, I…"

"You what?"

Words clogged his throat.

She smiled up at him, hair mussed and moonlight accentuating every curve hidden under her plain nightgown. "Don't you want to kiss your wife?"

Lord, he did, but he couldn't, not when he'd come here to end their marriage. "Can you wake your father for me?"

She scowled. "What's going on, Frank?"

Reluctantly, he stepped back. They were outside, yet it felt like walls were closing in on him from every angle.

"Frank, whatever it is, you can talk to me." She kissed his cheek, soft and nurturing, and his eyes closed. "I'm here for you," she whispered, breath warm across his jaw.

His mouth found hers. "Evie." Deep satisfaction rolled through him, primal and proud, when she kissed him back. She was his. And he wasn't ready to let her go.

"I knew you'd come back to me," she whispered, her voice full of trusting innocence he didn't have the heart to shatter.

He swallowed, confused and unable to see his plan through. "I was wrong, Evie. But I promise to make it up to you. I'm going to find a place for us to live, and we're going to do this right. I just need a little more time."

She hugged him, as if his assurance was all she needed. "I can wait—as long as it takes, Franklin. I have faith in you."

At least someone did.

CHAPTER 11

Over the next few weeks, Evie and Franklin had settled into a strange sort of marriage that wasn't much different from her days of being single. He visited at night, but never came inside.

Her father didn't say much, but she believed he was slowly coming to accept their union, even if he wasn't happy about how it started.

"Daddy's a forgiving man," she told Franklin one night as he sat on the porch swing with him. "I have faith that you two will be very close one day. He's always wanted a son."

Frank's brow creased. "I can't blame him for feeling the way he does. We disobeyed his wishes and I've made a mess of your life."

She nuzzled close to his side. "I don't mind messy. As long as I have you, I'm content."

"You're too understanding."

She snickered. "That's not true. You've seen my stubborn side."

He held her hand, and Evie smiled at the sight of their entwined fingers, admiring the way their wedding bands glinted in the moonlight. That porch swing was the most privacy they had of late, but she would take any chance she had to be close to Franklin. And she loved that he was now being more open with her about his feelings.

Without a doubt, she believed that if they faced their problems together, they could overcome and challenge. And boy, were they tested.

Her mother often said, there was usually a great big storm before any blessing. Evie prayed daily, accepting that this might not be *her* plan, but it was probably His. And she trusted God to see them through. They were just in a bit of a rainy season.

Things were starting to fall into place when another storm threw them off course. Evie had been hanging laundry on the line when Franklin came speeding up the drive, dust clouds billowing behind him like a hurricane whipping across the Georgia plains.

She instantly knew something was wrong. He never drove that fast, and it was barely past noon. He should have been at the dairy farm for hours yet.

Dropping a wet sheet into the basket, she hurried to meet him out front. "What's wrong?"

He held up a familiar yellow paper. "Another foreclosure notice! Now, they're taking the farm! They're taking everything I own. How am I ever going to pay down my father's debts if I can't make a living?"

Her heart plummeted. "But they offered the extension—"

"On the house. The farm is separate. I found a stack of notices in Pop's drawer, all unopened." He raked his fingers through his hair. "I'm never going to get out from under this."

"That's not true. There's always a solution. We just have to find it." She led him to the porch swing and urged him to sit. She rubbed his back, his muscles tense under her touch and his breathing unsteady.

"Lord have mercy, Evie. What have I done? I've married you, and I can't even provide a roof over our heads."

She tried to remain calm. "We'll figure it out. There has to be something—"

"There's nothing!" His voice rose in desperation. "I'm sorry. I'm not angry at you. I'm angry at him. Even from the grave, he's still making trouble for everyone he was supposed to protect."

"Being angry with him won't help matters."

"I know. I'm just…frustrated. I've sold what little I own to make the late payments and regain some of the bank's trust, but this is simply too much. If they take the farm, I'm lost."

"Show me the farm," she said softly.

He frowned in confusion. "What?"

"Show it to me. I want to see whatever it is that seems so irreplaceable to you."

An hour later, they stood on a pasture overlooking fields dotted by wooden structures. Thankfully, the perfume from the magnolia trees overpowered the stench of livestock on the wind.

They walked the property as the sun began to set, painting the sky in shades of peach and gold. Franklin pointed out the barn where he'd learned to milk cows, the pastures where the herd grazed, the creek that meandered through the property like a silver ribbon, providing fresh water year-round. His voice grew stronger as he talked about the land itself, his love for this place evident in every word.

"It's a good operation," he said, stopping beside the fence that overlooked the rolling hills dotted with live oaks. "The herd is healthy, and the land…Well, I know it's not much to look at, but it's what I know."

Nostalgia seemed to filter his view. Looking out, all she saw were dilapidated buildings and fences overdue for upkeep. But the cows looked happy. "I suppose this is what they call free range?"

"That's right."

If the bank did take the property, it likely wouldn't stay a farm. The Crossing was just around the bend, and the harbor would make much more money as a small community. She could see them dividing it up and selling it off in smaller parcels for single-family homes. They would make more money than they ever could collecting whatever the Prescotts still owed on their loan, and for that reason alone, she knew they likely wouldn't offer any extensions.

She knew then, Frank was out of a job. "Maybe I could find work in town," she suggested. "I can type or waitress."

"No." Franklin's voice was firm as an old oak. "I won't have my wife paying for my mistakes."

"They're not your mistakes, Franklin."

"Aren't they?" He looked at her with haunted eyes. "I should have known this would happen the moment they posted that first notice on the house." He bowed his head and wouldn't meet her eyes. "I've been thinking," he said quietly. "About us. About what's fair."

A chill ran down her spine like cold water from the creek. "What do you mean?"

When he finally looked at her, her heart race with fear. "I can't provide for you, Evie. I have no home to offer you, no steady income, no future worth speaking of. You married me thinking I was a man who could take care of his family, but I'm a failure, just like my father."

"Franklin Prescott, don't you dare—"

"We could have the marriage annulled," he continued as if she hadn't spoken. "You could find someone worthy of you, someone who could give you the life you deserve."

Tears sprang to her eyes, but they weren't tears of sadness. "How dare you? How dare you make that decision for me?"

Franklin blinked, surprised by her fierce tone.

"I didn't marry your dairy farm, Franklin! Nor did I marry your father's reputation! I married *you*. And when I tied my future to yours, I did so knowing full well it was forever, in sickness or health, through rich times or poor."

"But Evie—"

"No." Her voice was as firm as her faith. "We took vows before God. For better or worse. Did you think those were just pretty words?"

Franklin stared at her, something shifting in his expression. "I'm only trying to make things right."

"By giving me away to some other man? I love you, you fool! Not your farm, not your money, but your heart, your strength, and your goodness. If you think I'd let you walk away from your promises, you don't know me very well. I might be a Prescott by name, but us Caldwells are too stubborn to give up when we want something. And I've never wanted anything like I want you and this marriage."

He blinked in silence, as if afraid to speak. "What if I can't get the farm back?"

"Then we'll build a new one. Together."

"What if I fail?"

"Then it would prove you're human. You wouldn't be the first man to bite off more than he can chew."

He pulled her into his arms, knocking the wind out of her. "I love you so much," he whispered against her hair. "I don't deserve you."

"Then it's a good thing marriage isn't about deserving. It's about love and honoring our commitments. Now, take me home. The smell of manure is starting to waft in the heat."

"Yes, ma'am." As they walked back to the truck, hand in hand, Evie felt something shift between them. The crisis wasn't over, but her husband was finally starting to understand he wasn't facing these challenges alone. And that made all the difference in the world.

CHAPTER 12

The next morning brought a renewed sense of purpose that surprised them both. Franklin woke before dawn, not with the heavy despair that had plagued him for weeks, but with something that felt remarkably like hope.

"I've been approaching this all wrong," he told Evie over lunch the following day.

She set down her fork, studying her husband's face. "What do you mean?"

"What if I sold the farm, paid back my father's debt with the profit, cleared the Prescott name, and started fresh?"

"Could you do that?"

He shrugged. "The properties worth far more than the lean. Why should I let them make a profit at my expense?"

The idea was radical, and it scared them both. But as Franklin explained his thinking, Evie found herself caught up in his excitement.

"I've been running that dairy farm since I was sixteen," he continued, too excited to eat. "I know every inch of the operation and every customer's preferences. The knowledge doesn't disap-

109

pear just because the land does. The Morrison place has been sitting empty since old Mr. Morrison passed last year. His son lives up in Atlanta and has no interest in farming. The land is good, there's a decent barn, and the price is reasonable."

"How reasonable?"

He reached across the table to take her hands. "I still have something valuable to offer, years of experience and a reputation for honest dealing. Half the dairy farmers in this county have asked me for advice at one time or another. I could take on a silent partner, maybe even Morrison's son, if he's interested."

Over the following weeks, Franklin threw himself into his new plan with an energy that amazed everyone who knew him. He spent his days visiting neighboring farms, talking to potential investors, and scouting every abandoned inch of the old Morrison property.

The breakthrough came when Evie told Callie about Franklin's plan. Twenty-four hours later, Boone Whitmore approached his best friend with an unexpected offer.

It was exactly the kind of opportunity Franklin had been praying for, but he needed time to think it through carefully. That evening, he and Evie walked the Morrison property together, discussing the possibilities and challenges.

"It would mean starting over completely," Franklin warned as they strolled alongside the bay where the sweet magnolias were in full bloom. "Long hours, uncertain income for the first year or two, no guarantees of success."

"Would you be doing what you love?" Evie asked.

"Yes."

She took in the expansive openness on this side of The Crossing, her eyes once again drifting to space where she'd imagined a beautiful house overlooking the bay. "Would we be building something together, something that's truly ours?"

Franklin stopped walking and turned to face his wife. "Yes."

"Then what are we waiting for?"

The negotiations took another week, but by the end of August, Franklin and Boone had signed the partnership agreement. The Prescott-Whitmore Dairy was officially born, better known to its clients as P&W Farms.

Three days after listing his family's property, a developer made an offer to build an entire neighborhood of single-family homes. Frank couldn't sign the papers fast enough, and once that check cleared, the bank was paid, and they were on their way to their new home.

The physical work of transforming the Morrison place into a functioning dairy farm was backbreaking, but Franklin approached it with the joy of a man who'd found his purpose again. Every morning before dawn, he and Boone worked alongside hired hands to repair fences, upgrade the milking equipment, and prepare the pastures for their new herd.

Evie threw herself into the project with equal enthusiasm. She organized the old farmhouse they were temporarily staying in while their future home was getting built. It wasn't much, but at least they were finally under the same roof, as husband and wife should be.

Evie offered any support she could. She established a line of credit with local feed suppliers, and even designed simple advertisements for the P&W Farms in Blessings Harbor's newspaper.

"Prescott-Whitmore Dairy: Fresh, Local, Family-Owned," she read proudly, showing Franklin the draft one evening as they sat together on the front porch of their new home.

"I love it," Franklin said, pulling her close. "Though I think you should add 'Wife-Managed' to that list."

The cows arrived that September, twenty-five healthy Holstein dairy cattle that Franklin had personally selected from farms across the county. Watching them graze in their new pasture, her husband glowed with satisfaction far deeper than anything he'd experienced during his years trying to save his father's failing operation.

"They look content," Evie observed, joining him at the fence.

"They should be. This is good land, and they'll be well cared for." Franklin wrapped his arm around her waist. "I know it's not the grand legacy I hoped for, but it's honest work we're building together."

"It's better than a legacy," Evie said softly. "It's a foundation."

By October, they were producing enough milk to supply three restaurants in Blessings Harbor and had a growing list of residential customers who appreciated the quality and freshness of their product. Franklin's reputation for reliability and fair dealing, established during his years at the family farm, served them well in building customer loyalty.

The financial pressures were still significant—every penny of profit went back into expanding the operation—but Franklin no longer carried the crushing weight of inherited debt and shame. He was building something new, something clean, something entirely his own.

The transformation in him was remarkable. The hesitant, guilt-ridden man who'd almost walked away from their marriage had been replaced by a confident businessman who approached each challenge with determination and optimism.

"The house should be finished soon." Franklin said one evening as they reviewed the day's sales figures at their kitchen table.

Evie's heart swelled with pride and love. Glancing out the window of the old farmhouse, her gaze went to her favorite spot that overlooked Sweet Magnolia Bay. "A place where our family can grow." Her hand instinctively moving to her flat stomach.

"Our family," he repeated softly, catching the gesture. His jaw dropped. "Evie?"

She smiled. "I tried to wait, but, well…It's your fault really."

He laughed and danced her across the room, more animated than she ever saw him act. "What do you think about dormer windows in the children's rooms?" he'd ask, or "Should we plan for a large kitchen, in case we have lots of little ones to feed?"

She laughed with him. "Unless you plan on never touching me again, I'd plan for lots of little ones."

He kissed her, dropping his hand to her flat belly as he whispered, "You're gonna be an amazing mama."

"And you're going to be an incredible daddy."

CHAPTER 13

ow that they had a baby on the way, Franklin rushed to complete the house. The morning sickness came gently at first, just a touch of queasiness that made her push away her breakfast every now and then.

"You feeling poorly again, darlin'?" Franklin set down his coffee cup, his brow creased with worry. "Maybe we should have Dr. Burke take a look at you."

Evie managed a weak smile, one hand pressed to her stomach. "I'm sure it's nothing serious. My appetite's just changing. I don't think she cares for grits."

"She?" Franklin smiled.

Evie blushed. "I know there's no way of knowing for certain, but something tells me she's a girl. I've been craving strawberries constantly, and they're so pink and sweet." She paused, suddenly shy. "What do you think of the name Mary, after my mother?"

"Mary," he repeated softly. "Mary Prescott. Sounds perfect, sweetheart. Just perfect." He gave her hand a squeeze. "We'll move into the new house before the baby comes."

115

The house was going to be larger than either of them had planned or dared dream. Franklin had designed it with their future family in mind, including plenty of bedrooms for the children they hoped to have and a large kitchen where they could all gather for meals.

"The nursery will face east," he explained. "Morning light is best for babies. And I want only the best for ours."

As the weeks progressed, Evie bloomed. The morning sickness faded, replaced by a serene contentment that seemed to glow from within. Franklin was endlessly protective, insisting she rest more and refusing to let her lift anything heavier than a teacup.

"You're carrying our precious child," he'd say whenever she protested his hovering. "That's the most important work in the world."

The community rallied around Evie with advice and gifts, sharing stories of their own children and grandchildren. Glory appointed herself unofficial godmother, stopping by regularly with salty treats and items for the hope chest.

Franklin threw himself into preparing for fatherhood with characteristic determination. He crafted a beautiful crib by hand, sanding every surface to a silk-smooth finish. He also began working on a rocking chair, spending evenings in his workshop while Evie rested by the fire.

"I want everything perfect for Mary," he explained when Evie found him still working by lamplight one cold autumn evening. "She deserves the very best we can give her."

Their new house would be completed just before Thanksgiving, and Evie couldn't wait to move their belongings from the old farmhouse to their new home on the ridge. By that time, she expected to be showing.

Evie felt more content than she'd ever imagined possible. Their love, their home, their thriving business, and their coming child created a perfect circle of blessing that felt like a glimpse of heaven itself. The foundation they'd built together was stronger than either of them had ever imagined, their love unshakable.

Little did they know how much they'd need their strength in months to come.

CHAPTER 14

$\mathscr{A}$ cold snap that kept everyone in Blessings Harbor inside that autumn, which was fine by Evie, sine her back had been hurting lately.

"How bad could it be?" Callie asked. "You're not even showing yet."

"Not all pregnancy symptoms are tied to the baby bump, Callie."

Her sister rolled her eyes. "Should we expect this much drama every time you're in this predicament."

Evie bit into her pickle. "Yes."

Her back was still aching when Franklin came home, and he insisted she lie down. She must have been exhausted, because she fell right to sleep. But later that evening, Evie awoke with cramping that felt different from anything she'd experienced before. She lay in bed for several minutes, trying to convince herself it was normal, but when she stood up, a sharp pain doubled her over.

"Evie?" Franklin was beside her in an instant, his face filled with concern as he helped her sit on the edge of the bed. "What's wrong, sweetheart?"

"Something doesn't feel right," she whispered, one hand pressed to her abdomen. "There's…" She hissed in a sharp breath. "Call Dr. Burke."

His face went paled as he rushed to the phone. The doctor came right over to check her out, but as he listened for the baby's heartbeat with his stethoscope, his expression grew increasingly grave, and by the end of the night, her worst fears had been realized.

Evie was inconsolable, and Frank was at a loss. He called her mother, but even she couldn't break through her grief.

"There will be others," her mother whispered, but her well intentioned words only made Evie cry.

The physical process was mercifully compared to the emotional fallout she suffered. In the space of a few hours, all their dreams and plans for their first child had been swept away.

"She was real," Evie whispered to Frank the following night when he took away her untouched supper.

"I know she was. And she was ours."

A tear slid from the corner of her eye into her hair. "Mary," she whispered, her voice raw from crying. "Mary Prescott."

Franklin knelt beside the bed, his eyes red with unshed tears, his strong face marked by a grief that matched her own. "She'll always be our sweet Mary," he said softly. "Our little girl."

THE DAYS FOLLOWING THE LOSS OF MARY PASSED IN A BLUR OF grief and well-meaning visitors. The church ladies brought food and flowers, Pastor Mark offered gentle words about God's mysterious plan, and friends stopped by to share their condolences. But nothing could touch the profound emptiness that had settled over

Frank and Evie's home like Spanish moss draping the ancient oaks.

Evie barely spoke for the first week. She spent most of her time staring out at the bay, wondering if she'd ever feel excitement for anything again. Franklin watched her with growing concern, unsure how to comfort a grief so deep it seemed to have no bottom.

"She needs time," Glory advised one night when Frank expressed his worry for his wife. "Losing a child is like losing a piece of your own soul. There's no rushing that kind of healing."

He threw himself into the farm work, staying busy from dawn until dusk, but the physical labor couldn't quiet the ache in his chest. Every time he thought about the future they'd been planning, the loss hit him anew.

"I keep thinking about all the things I'll never get to do with her," Evie whispered one night as they lay in bed. "I'll never feel her kick, never hold her in my arms, never hear her voice."

Franklin turned to face her, his heart breaking at the pain in her voice. "I think about that too," he admitted. "I think about all the plans we made, all the dreams we had for her future."

They held each other and cried until there were no tears left, both struggling to understand how life could be so cruel, how God could give them such joy only to snatch it away so quickly.

THE WEEKS THAT FOLLOWED WERE THE DARKEST OF THEIR marriage. Some days, Evie couldn't bring herself to get out of bed. Other days, she cleaned the house frantically, as if staying busy could somehow outrun the grief. Franklin watched helplessly, wanting to comfort her but battling his own overwhelming sorrow.

It was Glory who finally helped them begin to heal, arriving one afternoon with a basket of gardening supplies and a determined expression.

"Come with me," she commanded, dragging them to the new property where their future home was being built. "Grief is like a garden. If you don't tend it properly, it either withers away to nothing or grows wild and chokes out everything else. You need to find a way to honor Mary's memory that brings life, not just sorrow."

Under Glory's guidance, Frank dug holes and Evie planted a small memorial garden beneath the kitchen window—roses for love, forget-me-nots for remembrance, and sweet alyssum for worth beyond beauty. As her hands worked in the soil, something began to shift in her heart.

"I would have taught her to garden, shown her how to make things grow," Evie said softly as she patted soil around a rosebush.

"She did make things grow," Glory replied. "She made love grow in your heart, and made you grow as a woman and a wife. That love doesn't disappear just because she's not here to see it, Evie."

For the first time since losing Mary, Evie's face looked peaceful rather than broken.

"Glory's right, darlin'. Mary changed us for the better. She made us see possibilities we couldn't imagine on our own." He lovingly traced a gentle finger down her cheek and she leaned into his touch. "You taught me to believe in second chances, Evie, and I know there will come a time when we feel whole again."

She looked up at him, smiling though tears filled her eyes. "I believe that too. But it's going to take time."

"We made vows, remember? You've got me forever. When the time comes, I'll be right here, by your side. The only place I ever want to be."

CHAPTER 15

year passed, and the seasons turned full circle since the loss of Mary, bringing healing in ways neither Franklin nor Evie could have imagined. Their memorial garden bloomed magnificently that first spring, drawing butterflies and hummingbirds that seemed to dance among the flowers in celebration of life. The three magnolias they planted on the ridge had grown taller and stronger, their branches reaching toward heaven as if carrying their prayers upward.

The Prescott-Whitmore Dairy had flourished beyond even Franklin's optimistic projections. Word had spread throughout Blessings Harbor and beyond about the quality of their milk and cream, and they now supplied not only local restaurants and families but also shipped to customers as far away as Savannah. Franklin had purchased additional acreage and expanded their herd to fifty head of prime Holstein cattle.

"We built something remarkable here," Boone observed one crisp October morning as they watched the cows grazing peacefully in the expanded pasture. "You should be proud of what you've accomplished."

Franklin nodded, but his eyes were on Evie, who was hanging laundry on the line behind their new house. She moved with a grace and contentment that spoke of healed hearts, though he sometimes caught her pausing in her work to gaze toward Mary's memorial grove.

"We've all grown stronger," Franklin replied, knowing that he and Evie weren't the only ones to face their fair share of challenges.

That evening, after Boone went home, Franklin looked up from the farm ledgers he'd been reviewing to find his wife watching him with an expression he couldn't quite read.

"Did I do something?"

Evie set down her needlework and moved to sit beside him on the sofa. "Actually, yes."

He set aside the ledger and faced her. "Let's have it." He hoped it was something minor, like leaving the cellar light on or forgetting to put down the seat. She didn't look particularly cross with him, so he assumed it was a minor infraction.

"We're out of paint."

"Paint?"

"Yes. I'm not sure if pink or blue is right this time, so I was thinking yellow or green."

He frowned. "I'm lost. What are we—" He words cut off when she smiled. He'd seen that smile before, one that said she had the greatest secret to share. He was almost afraid to ask. "Evie, darlin', are you trying to tell me…"

Her smile stretched. "Yes, Frank. It's happened again. I saw Dr. Burke this afternoon."

He laughed. "And you're happy?"

"Beyond happy. I'm elated."

He hugged her tight, gratitude and a deep sense of welcomed

responsibility washing over him. "How... how far along?" he managed.

"About two months. Due sometime in late spring." Her voice grew stronger. " Dr. Burke says everything looks very good. My health's excellent, and he sees no reason for concern."

He gathered her in his arms, holding her close as he struggled with emotions too complex to name.

"Are you happy?" she asked quietly.

"Terrified and happy," he admitted against her shoulder. "But more happy than terrified."

"Me too."

That night, they knelt together and prayed.

The pregnancy progressed beautifully. Evie felt strong and energetic, with only the mildest morning sickness that passed quickly. Dr. Burke monitored her carefully, but each visit brought reassurance that mother and baby were thriving.

"I can feel her moving," Evie announced one February evening as they sat by the fire. At four months along, her pregnancy was beginning to show, and the baby's movements had become a source of daily wonder.

"Her?" Franklin smiled, resting his hand where Evie indicated the movement. "You're certain it's a girl again?"

"A mother has a sense about such things," she informed. "How do you feel about the name Caroline? The baby books say it means 'strong and beautiful,' which is exactly what I pray she'll be."

"I think that's a perfect name for our little girl."

The following May, Caroline Rose Prescott made her entrance into the world. Evie wept with joy as Dr. Burke placed their daughter in her arms. The baby was rosy-cheeked and alert, with a cap of golden hair and blue eyes like her father. She quieted immediately at her mother's touch, as if recognizing the voice she'd heard for nine months.

"Hello, my little sweet pea," Evie whispered, touching Caroline's tiny hand. "We've waiting so long to meet you."

Franklin stood beside the bed, overwhelmed by emotions too powerful for words. "She's beautiful, like her mother," he finally managed.

"And she has her father's strength," Evie added, marveling at Caroline's firm grip on her finger. "She's going to be a force to be reckoned with."

He laughed, recalling the words her father once said to him. "She'll be a good girl."

Evie looked up at him and laughed. "You don't look so sure, Frank. As a matter of fact, you look terrified."

He'd never thought he could love anyone as much as he loved Evie, but now there were two females in his life and he felt the crushing responsibility to protect them. "There must be magic in your blood, darlin', because I already love her far more than I ever imagined."

Glory arrived within hours, bringing soup and practical advice along with her warm congratulations. She took one look at baby Caroline and nodded approvingly.

Word spread quickly through Blessings Harbor that the Prescotts had welcomed their first child. Friends and neighbors stopped by with gifts and well-wishes, sharing in the joy that seemed to radiate from the farmhouse on the ridge.

As the summer weeks passed, Caroline proved to be an easy, happy baby. She slept well, nursed eagerly, and seemed to find contentment in the rhythm of farm life. Franklin would carry her in his arms as he did the evening chores, pointing out the cows and explaining the work of the dairy farm.

"Someday you'll help Daddy with the milking," he'd tell her as she gazed up at him with serious blue eyes. "But for now, you just focus on growing big and strong."

Evie divided her time between caring for Caroline and helping with the administrative tasks at the farm. She didn't mind working, but she would always prefer motherhood first.

The christening took place on a perfect Sunday in July, with the entire congregation of Blessings Harbor Community Church in attendance. Caroline wore a christening gown that Evie had sewn by hand, embroidered with tiny rosebuds and trimmed with lace that had belonged to Franklin's mother.

As Pastor Mark held Caroline over the baptismal font, she gurgled happily, reaching for the drops of water with chubby fingers that made the congregation chuckle.

"Caroline Rose Prescott," Pastor Mark declared, "I baptize you in the name of the Father, and of the Son, and of the Holy Spirit. May you grow in wisdom and grace, surrounded by the love of family and community."

After the service, the entire church gathered at the Prescott farm for a celebration dinner. Tables were set up under the shade trees, loaded with dishes prepared by neighbors. Children ran through the pastures while the adults shared stories and laughter.

"Watch out for steaming divots," Boone yelled, and Callie swatted him in the arm.

"You've got yourself a fine home here," Rawlin observed, staring over The Crossing toward the bay where the sweet magnolias bloomed.

"More houses are being built. There's still time for you and Glory to move closer."

"She reminds me every day," his friend joked.

"It's a good life," Boone agreed, having just moved himself and Callie into one of the new houses on the other side of The Crossing.

"Better than I ever dared hope for," Franklin agreed.

As evening approached and the guests departed, Franklin and Evie found themselves alone on their front porch, sipping sweet tea as their sleeping daughter dozed quietly in the bassinette. The sunset painted the sky over the bay in shades of pink and gold, and the air was sweet with the scent of honeysuckle and magnolia blossoms.

"Do you remember our wedding day?" Evie asked, resting her head on his shoulder as they rocked slowly on the porch swing.

"Every detail." He drew circles over her knee where their legs touched. "You in that borrowed dress, promising to love me for better or worse."

"We're very blessed," she said, tracing the gold band around his finger.

He glanced at her as blue moonlight shadowed her features. Stars appear in the darkening sky, blanketing them in peaceful silence. She seemed to have something to say, but was having a difficult time getting it out.

"It's not like you to sit in silence, Evie. What's on your mind?"

Her hand curled around his as she pressed a kiss to his cheek. "I was thinking how important it is to have sisters."

"You've got two of the best."

She smiled. "Maybe it's time we give Caroline one."

He drew back. "So soon?"

She shrugged. "It's not like it's a chore."

He laughed. "That it isn't." Pressing a kiss to her temple, he said, "Why don't you head up and I'll put this little blessing to bed. Then we can see about making your wish come true."

CHAPTER 16

One year later, the Prescott family had grown again.

Evie stood at the kitchen window, watching Franklin play with Caroline in the front yard as her hand curved lovingly around her swollen belly, certain this one was a boy.

"Your sister has your daddy wrapped around her little finger," she whispered, smiling as the two twirled and Caroline's squealing laughter carried over the bay.

When they finally came inside for something to drink, Frank was out of breath. "Is he kicking?" he asked, coming to press a hand to her belly.

"A little."

He smiled when the baby gave a firm thump. "Caleb the kicker," he joked.

Caleb Franklin Prescott, she thought, thinking the name had a nice ring to it.

Frank opened the fridge in search of sweet tea, but was distracted by the sampling of their newest cheese. The dairy farm had continued to prosper beyond their wildest dreams. They now employed a crew of full-time workers and supplied dairy products to customers throughout coastal Georgia. They were expanding into cheese production after receiving numerous requests from restaurants in Savannah for locally-made specialty cheeses.

He popped a sample of Gouda in his mouth and moaned.

"Don't spoil your supper."

He stole a cut of cheddar and then returned the plate to the fridge. Caroline bounced with curiosity, and he gave her a small piece to sample.

"That's enough," Evie said, steering them both toward the sink. "Wash up for dinner."

Little Caleb made his debut on a crisp October morning, arriving with none of the drama that had surrounded Caroline's birth. He was a sturdy, healthy baby boy, with dark hair like his father's and a surprisingly calm disposition for one who'd been so active in the womb.

"He's beautiful," Franklin whispered as he held his son for the first time. "Look at those hands—he's going to be a worker, like his daddy."

"And look at those eyes," Evie added, noting the serious way Caleb seemed to study his surroundings. "He's already taking everything in."

Caroline was fascinated by her new brother, insisting on helping with everything from diaper changes to feeding time. She would sit beside Evie during nursing sessions, patting Caleb's head gently and singing the lullabies she'd learned.

"Baby," she's say, peppering Caleb with kisses. "My baby."

"Your baby brother," Evie would tell her. "You're his big sister, so it's your job to love and protect him."

"Yes, Mama."

Evie always said she wanted a large family, but some folks

found it difficult to believe how large. Eight little ones was just about perfect, though in Blessings Harbor, unexpected blessings had a way of showing up when you least expected them.

The Crossing at Sweet Magnolia Bay had become the exact sort of home she'd dreamed it could be, filled to the rafters with love and laughter, evenings on the front porch sipping sweet tea, and long Sunday suppers with plenty of family. Their home was the sort of place everyone considered home. Even Evie's father, despite his rocky start with Franklin, said it was the kind of home dreams were made of. The day he told her that, she confessed, "It was my dream, Daddy, and Frank made it for me."

"He's a good man, Evie."

Nothing made her happier than to hear her father admit such a truth. "Yes, he certainly is." She didn't want to offend her father, but Frank was probably the best man she knew. There wasn't much he couldn't do, and he loved her more than anyone else ever had. "I suppose that's the closest you'll ever come to admitting you were wrong."

Her father scowled at her, but didn't disagree. "Hush now and drink your tea. The sun's about to set and I don't want to miss it."

She smirked as she sipped from her glass. Frank, standing on the dock with the boys, looked back at her and grinned. They gathered for the sunset nearly every night. She loved the way it reflected over the soft ripples of the bay almost as much as she loved her life here at The Crossing.

Every corner of their home whispered stories built of love, laughter, faith, and family, but the best chapters were yet to come. She had no doubt that each one of her children would have a story of their own to tell, and her sisters' children, and their children's children. All because two hearts crossed paths one wild day at a café near Sweet Magnolia Bay.

THE END
...For Now...

My goodness, that was fun!
Let's do it again real soon. Caroline's Story is next!
Click here to go to the next book in Blessings Harbor,
The Crossing at Sweet Magnolia Bay: Grant & Caroline!

Click HERE to sign up for my newsletter, Sweet Tea with Josie, so that we can keep in touch!

You can also find me on Facebook & Instagram!
And, hey, if you're feelin' social, join my Reader Group HERE!

Hey Sugar,
Keep in Touch, Now...

Connect With Josie Collins

www.JosieCollins.com
Website

@AuthorJosieCollins
Instagram

Josie Collins
Facebook

Sweet Tea With Josie
Newsletter

Facebook
Reader Group

There's so much more to share from Blessings Harbor! Keep an eye out for Caroline's story next!

ABOUT JOSIE COLLINS

Swoon, smile, and stay a while...

Josie Collins writes clean and wholesome Southern romance with sweet Christian undertones and small-town charm. A lifelong daydreamer with a soft spot for second chances and front porch love stories, she's the heart behind the *Blessings Harbor* series, where faith, hope, and happy endings bloom like magnolias in spring.

When she's not writing, you'll find Josie sipping sweet tea, flipping through old family recipes, or curled up with a good book and her favorite quilt. She believes in the power of kindness, the beauty of simple things, and the kind of love that feels like home.

If you enjoy stories full of heart, hope, and homegrown romance,
Josie's books just might be your next favorite escape.